Three Margarets

Laura Elizabeth Howe Richards

Three Margarets
Copyright © 2024 Bibliotech Press
All rights reserved

The present edition is a reproduction of previous publication of this classic work. Minor typographical errors may have been corrected without note; however, for an authentic reading experience the spelling, punctuation, and capitalization have been retained from the original text.

ISBN: 979-8-88830-910-0

CONTENTS

Chapter I	The Arrival		1
Chapter II	First Thoughts		8
Chapter III	The White Lady of Fernley		17
Chapter IV	Confidence		25
Chapter V	The Peat-bog		33
Chapter VI	The Family Chest		41
Chapter VII	The Garret		51
Chapter VIII	Cuba Libre		60
Chapter IX	Day by Day		68
Chapter X	Looking Backward		76
Chapter XI	Heroes and Heroines		85
Chapter XII	In the Saddle		98
Chapter XIII	In the Night		109
Chapter XIV	Explanations		115
Chapter XV	Farewell		123

CHAPTER I

THE ARRIVAL

> Long ago and long ago,
> And long ago still,
> There dwelt three merry maidens
> Upon a distant hill.
>
> Christina G. Rossetti.

The rain was falling fast. It was a pleasant summer rain that plashed gently on the leaves of the great elms and locusts, and tinkled musically in the roadside puddles. Less musical was its sound as it drummed on the top of the great landau which was rolling along the avenue leading to Fernley House; but the occupants of the carriage paid little attention to it, each being buried in her own thoughts. The night was dark, and the carriage-lamps threw an uncertain gleam on the three figures leaning back in their corners, muffled and silent. The avenue was long,—interminably long, it seemed to one of the three travellers; and finally the silence so oppressed her that she determined to conquer her shyness and break it.

"What a very long avenue!" she said, speaking in a low, sweet voice.

There was no reply. She hesitated a moment, and then added timidly, "Don't you think that, as we are cousins, we might introduce ourselves and make acquaintance? My name is Margaret Montfort."

"Why, so is mine!" exclaimed the traveller opposite her. "And mine!" added the third, from the further corner.

The voice of the second speaker sounded as if it might be hearty, and as if only awkwardness gave it a sullen tone. The third spoke with a soft, languid utterance and the faintest shade of a foreign accent.

"How strange!" exclaimed the first Margaret Montfort. "Of course I knew that we had the same surname, as our fathers were brothers; but that we should all three be named—and yet it is not strange, after all!" she added. "Our grandmother was Margaret, and it was natural that we should be given her name. But how shall we manage? We cannot say First, Second, and Third Margaret, as they do on the stage."

"I am never called anything but Peggy," said the second girl, still in a half-sullen, half-timid tone.

And "My home name is Rita," murmured the third reluctantly; and she added something in an undertone about "short acquaintance," which the first Margaret did not choose to hear.

"Oh, how pretty!" she said cordially. "Then I may call you Peggy and Rita? About myself"—she stopped and laughed—"I hardly know what to say, for I have always been called Margaret, since I was a baby."

"But one of us might as well be Margaret," answered Peggy. "And somehow, your voice sounds as if you looked like it. If this road were ever coming to an end, we might see."

"Oh, I do see!" cried Margaret, leaning forward to look out of the window. "I see the lights! I see the house! We are really here at last!"

As she spoke, the carriage drove up before a long building twinkling with lights, and stopped at a broad flight of steps, leading to a stone-paved veranda. As the coachman opened the carriage-door, the door of the house opened too, and a cheerful light streamed out upon the three weary travellers. Two staid waiting-women, in spotless caps and aprons, were waiting to receive them as they came up the steps.

"This way, young ladies, if you please!" said the elder of the two.

"You must be tired with your long drive. This is the library; and will you rest here a while, or will you be shown your rooms at once?"

"Oh, thank you!" said Margaret, "let us stay here a little while! What do you say, cousins?"

"All right!" said Peggy. The girl whose home name was Rita had already thrown herself down in an armchair, and seemed to think no reply necessary.

"Very well, miss," said the dignified waiting-woman, addressing herself markedly to Margaret. "Susan will come in ten minutes to show you the rooms, miss, and supper will be ready in half an hour. I am Elizabeth, miss, if you should want me. The bell is here in the corner."

Margaret thanked her with a cordial smile, the other two never glancing in her direction, and the woman withdrew.

"Just ten minutes," said Margaret, turning to her cousins, "to make acquaintance in, and find out what we all look like! Suppose we begin by taking off our wraps. How delightful the little fire is, even if we are in the middle of June. Let me help you, Peggy!"

Peggy was fumbling at her veil, which was tied in a hard knot; but in a few minutes everything was off, and the three Margaret Montforts stood silent, gazing at each other.

Nearest the fire stood the girl who was called Peggy. She was apparently about sixteen, plump and fair, with a profusion of blonde hair which looked as if it were trying to fly away. Her round, rosy cheeks, blue eyes, and pouting lips gave her a cherubic contour which was comically at variance with her little tilted nose; but she was pretty, in spite of her singularly ill-devised and ill-fitting costume of green flannel.

Reclining in the armchair next her, the Margaret who was called Rita was a startling contrast to the rosy Peggy. She was a year older, slight and graceful, her simple black gown fitting like a glove and saying "Paris" in every seam. Her hair was absolutely black, her eyes large and dark, her delicate features regular and finely cut; but the beautiful face wore an expression of discontent, and there were two fine vertical lines between the eyebrows. Her complexion had the clear pallor of a Cape Jessamine.

Facing these two, and looking with thoughtful eyes from one to the other, stood the girl whom we have spoken of as the first Margaret. She was seventeen, within two months of the age of her dark-eyed cousin. Lacking the brilliant colouring of the other two, her face had its own charm. Her eyes were dark gray, with violet shades in them, deepened by the long and heavy black lashes. The faint tinge of colour in her smooth cheeks was that of the wild rose; her wavy chestnut hair had glints of gold here and there in it, and though her nose was nothing in particular, she had the prettiest mouth in the world, and a dimple beside it. In conclusion, she was dressed in dark blue, simply, yet tastefully too.

"Well," said Peggy, breaking the silence with an embarrassed giggle, "I hope we shall know each other the next time we meet."

Margaret blushed. "I fear I have been staring rudely!" she said. "But I have never had any cousins before,—never seen any, that is, and I am really so glad to know you both! Let us shake hands, girls, and try to be friends!"

She spoke so pleasantly that Peggy's plump hand and Rita's delicate white fingers were at once extended. Holding them in her own, Margaret hesitated a moment, and then, bending forward, kissed both girls timidly on the cheek.

"Our fathers were own brothers," she said. "We must try to be fond of each other. And now," she added, "let us all tell our tales, as the children say. Rita, you shall begin. Tell us about yourself and your home, and anything else that you will."

Rita settled herself comfortably in her chair, and looked meditatively at the tip of her little boot.

"My home," she said, "is in Havana. My mother was a Spaniard, a San Real. My father is Richard Montfort. My mother died three years ago, and my father has lately married again, a girl of my own age. You may imagine that I do not find home particularly attractive now, so I was glad to accept my Uncle John's invitation to spend the summer here. As I have money in my own right, I was at liberty to do as I pleased; nor in truth did my father object, but the contrary. I have never seen my uncle."

"Nor I!" "Nor I!" exclaimed the other two.

"But I received this note from him a month ago."

She produced a note from her reticule, and read as follows.

> "My dear Niece:
>
> The thought has occurred to me that it would be well for you to make some acquaintance with the home of your fathers. I therefore invite you to spend the coming summer here, with the daughters of my brothers James and Roger, to whom I have extended a similar invitation. Business will unhappily prevent me from receiving you in person, but my cousin and yours, Mrs. Cheriton, who resides at Fernley, will pay you every attention.
>
> Trusting that this plan will meet with your approval and that of your father,
>
> I am, my dear niece,
> Your affectionate uncle,
>
> John Montfort."

"Well, I never!" cried Peggy, drawing a long breath. "Why, it's word for word like my note."

"And like mine!" said Margaret.

The three notes were laid side by side, and proved to be exactly alike, even to the brief flourish under the signature; with the one difference that in Margaret's the words "and that of your father," were omitted.

"He must be a very methodical man!" said Margaret thoughtfully. "Isn't it strange that none of us has ever seen him? And yet one can understand how it has been. The other brothers, our fathers, left home when they were quite young,—that is what Papa has told me,—and soon formed ties elsewhere. Uncle John stayed with Grandfather till he died; then he went abroad, and was gone many years; and since he came back, he has lived here alone. I suppose he has grown a recluse, and does not care to see people. I know Papa often and often begged him to come and make us a visit, and once or twice the time was actually set; but each time something happened to prevent his coming, and he never did come. I think he would have come last year, when dear Papa died, but he had had some accident, and had injured his foot so that he could not walk."

"Pa read us the letter you wrote him then," said Peggy, with an awkward attempt at condolence. "He said he thought you must be a nice girl."

The tears came quickly to Margaret's eyes, and she turned her head to hide them. Peggy instantly plunged into a description of her nine brothers and sisters, and their life on the great Western farm where they lived; but she was hardly under way when the demure Susan tapped at the door, and said with gentle firmness that she had come to show the young ladies their rooms.

There was a sudden clutching of hats, cloaks, and bags, and the next moment the three maidens were ascending the wide staircase, casting looks of curiosity and wonderment about them.

"What beautiful twisted balusters!" whispered Margaret.

"And such queer old pictures!" said Peggy. "My! How they stare! Wondering who we are, I suppose."

Arrived in the wide upper hall, Susan threw open the doors of three rooms, two side by side, the third opposite.

"This is yours, Miss Montfort," she said. "This is the young lady's from the South, and this the other young lady's. Mr. Montfort arranged it all before he left."

"How kind and thoughtful!" cried Margaret.

"How precise and formal!" murmured Rita.

Peggy said nothing, but stared with round eyes. These rooms were not like the great whitewashed chamber at home, where she and her three sisters slept in iron bedsteads. These rooms were not large, but oh, so pretty and cosy! In each was an open fireplace, with a tiny fire burning,—"just for looks," Susan explained. Each contained a pretty brass bedstead, a comfortable chair or two, and curtains and cushions of flowered chintz. Rita's chintz showed deep red poppies on a pale buff ground;

Peggy's was blue, with buttercups and daisies scattered over it; while Margaret's—oh, Margaret's was not chintz after all, but old-fashioned white dimity, with a bewilderment of tufts, and ball-fringe, and tassels. Candles were lighted on the trim dressing-tables; everything was spotless, fresh, and inviting, and the three tired girls sank each into her soft-cushioned easy chair with a delightful sense of being at home.

"The tea-bell will ring in half an hour, if you please," said Susan, and she closed the three doors.

CHAPTER II

FIRST THOUGHTS

> "The eggs and the ham,
> And the strawberry jam;
> The rollicking bun,
> And the gay Sally Lunn."

"Ting! ting-a-ling!" the silver tinkle sounded cheerfully. Margaret was the first to leave her room, punctuality being the third virtue of her creed. She had changed her travelling-dress for a pretty dark red cashmere, which became her well; but Peggy, who came running down a moment later, still wore her ill-fitting frock of green flannel, the scant attractions of which were not enhanced by a soiled linen collar, which she had forgotten to change. The flyaway locks were indeed braided together, but the heavy braid was rough and uneven.

"Oh, you have changed your dress!" she cried, seeing Margaret. "How pretty you look! I didn't have time to do anything. Say," she added, lowering her voice, "I think you are sweet, but I just hate that other girl. We sha'n't be fond of each other, you may be sure of that!"

"My dear Peggy!" said Margaret, in gentle remonstrance. "You must not judge a person on ten minutes' acquaintance. I am sure I hope you and Rita will be very good friends. You certainly must admire her beauty."

"Oh, she's pretty enough!" rejoined Peggy; "but I think she's perfectly horrid!—there now! Stuck-up and conceited, and looking at other people as if they were stone posts. And I am not a stone post, you know."

"You certainly don't look like one," said Margaret, laughing; "nor feel like one," she added, putting her arm around her cousin's plump waist.

"But come! here is Elizabeth waiting to show us the dining-room. Elizabeth, we have had a good rest, and we are so hungry."

"This way, miss, if you please," said the grave Elizabeth. And she led the way across the hall. The dining-room was a pleasant square room, with crimson curtains closely drawn. There was no cloth on the dark table, which shone like a mirror, reflecting the blaze of the candles in mellow points of light. At the head stood a shining silver tea-service and a Dresden chocolate-pot, surrounded by the prettiest cups and saucers that ever were seen; and a supper was laid out which seemed to have been specially planned for three hungry girls. Everything good, and plenty of it.

"My!" whispered Peggy, "isn't this fine? But how funny to have no table-cloth! We always have a red one at supper."

"Do you?" said Margaret. "Papa always liked the bare table."

"Will you take the head of the table, miss?" asked Elizabeth. "I have set your place here, and Miss—"

"Miss Peggy's," suggested Margaret gently.

"Thank you, miss! Miss Peggy's at the side here."

"Very well," said Margaret. "We shall sit just where you put us, Elizabeth. And Miss Rita will sit opposite me and carve the chicken. Oh, here she is! Rita, are you accomplished in the art of carving?"

Rita, who now came gliding in, shook her head as she took the seat appointed her. "I have never attempted it," she said, "and don't think I care to try, thanks! Take this to the sideboard and carve it," she added, addressing Elizabeth in a tone of careless command. The woman obeyed in silence; but the quick colour sprang to Margaret's cheek, and she looked as much distressed as if the rude speech had been addressed to her.

Peggy stared. "Don't they say 'please' in Havana?" she said in a loud whisper to Margaret. But Margaret rattled the tea-cups, and pretended not to hear.

"Will you take tea, Rita, or chocolate?" she asked quickly.

"Chocolate, please," replied her cousin languidly. "I wonder if it will be fit to drink? One hears that everything of that sort is so frightfully adulterated in this country."

"It looks delicious," said Margaret, pouring out the smooth, brown liquid. "Do you see, girls, what lovely cups these are? Look, Rita, they are all different! I shall give you this delicate pink one, for it just matches your gown.

Such a pretty gown!" she added admiringly, glancing at the pale rose-coloured silk and rich lace that set off the clear pallor of Rita's complexion in a wonderful way.

"It is only a tea-gown!" said the latter carelessly. "I have brought no clothes to speak of. Yes, the cup does match it rather well, doesn't it?"

"And you, Peggy," said Margaret, "shall have this blue darling with the gold arabesques. Surely, anything would taste good out of such cups,—take care! Oh, my dear!"

Margaret sprang up and tried to recapture the cup which had just left her hand. But it was too late! Peggy had taken it quickly, grasping the edge of the saucer. Naturally, the saucer tilted up, the cup tilted over, and a stream of chocolate poured over her hand and arm, and descended into her lap, where it formed a neat brown pool with green flannel banks. Moreover, an auxiliary stream was meandering over the table, making rapid progress towards the rose-coloured silk and white lace.

With an angry exclamation of "Bête!" Rita pushed her chair back out of danger. Poor Peggy, after the first terrified "Ow!" as the hot chocolate deluged her, sat still, apparently afraid of making matters worse if she stirred. Margaret, after ringing the bell violently to call Elizabeth, promptly checked the threatening rivulet on the table with her napkin, and then, seizing Peggy's, proceeded to sop up the pool as well as she could.

"I never!" gasped the unhappy girl. "Why, I didn't do a thing! it just tipped right over!"

"It is too bad!" said Margaret, as sympathetically as she could, though her cousin did look so funny, it was hard to keep from smiling. "Oh, here is Elizabeth! Elizabeth, we have had an accident, and I fear Miss Peggy's dress is quite ruined. Can you think of anything to take the stains out?"

Elizabeth surveyed the scene with a practised eye.

"Hot soapsuds will be the best thing," she said. "If the young lady will come up with me at once, and take the frock off, I will see what can be done."

"Yes, do go with Elizabeth, dear!" urged

Margaret. "Nothing can be done till the dress is off."

And poor Peggy went off, hanging her head and looking very miserable.

Rita, as soon as her dress was out of danger, was able to see the affair in another light, and as her cousin left the room burst into a peal of silvery laughter.

"Oh, hush!" cried Margaret. "She will hear you, Rita!"

"And if she does?" replied Rita, drawing her chair up to the table again, and sipping her chocolate leisurely. "Acrobats expect to be laughed at, and certainly this was a most astonishing tour de force. Seriously, my dear," she added, seeing Margaret's troubled look, "how are we to take our Western cousin, if we do not treat her as a comic monstrosity? Is it possible that she is a Montfort? I shall call her Cousin Calibana, I think!"

She nibbled daintily at a macaroon, and went on: "It is a thing to be thankful for that the green frock is probably hopelessly ruined. I am quite sure it would have affected my nerves seriously if I had been obliged to see it every day.

Do they perhaps cut dresses with a mowing-machine in the West?" and she laughed again, a laugh so rippling and musical that it was a pity it was not good-natured.

Margaret listened in troubled silence. What could she say that would not at once alienate this foreign cousin, who seemed now inclined to friendliness with her? And yet she could not let poor Peggy go undefended. At last she said gently, yet with meaning, "Dear Rita, you make me tremble for myself. If you are so very severe in your judgments, who can hope to pass uncriticised?"

"You, ma cousine!" cried Rita. "But there is no question of you; you are of one's own kind! You are altogether charming. Surely you must see that this young person is simply impossible. Impossible!" she repeated with decision. "There is no other word for it."

"No," said Margaret, bravely, "I do not see that, Rita! She is shy and awkward, and I should think very young for her age. But she has an honest, good face, and I like her. Besides," she added, unconsciously repeating the argument she had used in defending Rita herself against Peggy's animadversions, "it is absurd to judge a person on half an hour's acquaintance."

"Oh, half an hour!" said Rita lightly; "half a lifetime! My judgments, chère cousine, are made at the first glance, and remain fixed."

"And are they always right?" asked Margaret, half amused and half vexed.

"They are right for me!" said Rita, nodding her pretty head. "That is enough."

She pushed her chair back, and coming to Margaret's side, laid her hand lightly on her shoulder.

"Chère cousine," she said, in a caressing tone, "you are so charming, I do hope you are not good. It is detestable to be good! Avoid it, très chère! believe me, it is impossible!"

"Are all the people in Havana bad?" asked Margaret, returning the caress, and resisting the impulse to shake the pretty, foolish speaker.

"All!" replied Rita cheerfully; "enchanting, delightful people; all bad! Oh, of course when one is old, that is another matter! Then one begins—"

"Was your mother bad, Rita?" asked Margaret quietly.

"My mother was an angel, do you hear? a saint!" cried the girl. And suddenly, without the slightest warning, she burst into a tropical passion of tears, and sobbed and wept as if her heart would break.

Poor Margaret! Decidedly this was not a pleasant evening for her. By the time she had soothed Rita, and tucked her up on the library sofa, with a fan and a vinaigrette, Peggy had come down again, in a state of aggrieved dejection, to finish her supper. A wrapper of dingy brown replaced the green frock; she too had been crying, and her eyes were red and swollen.

"I wish I was at home!" she said sullenly, as she ate her chicken and buttered her roll. "I wish I hadn't come here. I knew I should have a horrid time, but Pa made me come."

"Oh, don't say that, Peggy, dear!" said Margaret. "You are tired to-night, and homesick, that is all; and it was very unlucky about the dress, of course. To-morrow, when you have had a good night's rest, you will feel very differently, I know you will. Just think how delightful it will be to explore the house, and to roam about the garden, where your father and mine used to play when they were boys. Hasn't your father told you about the swing under the great chestnut-trees, and the summer-houses, and—"

"Oh, yes!" said Peggy, her eyes brightening. "And I was to look in the long summer-house for his initials, cut in the roof. Uncle Roger stood on Uncle John's shoulders, and Pa on his; and when he was finishing the tail of the M, Pa gave such a dig with his knife that he lost his balance, and they all tumbled down together; and Pa has the mark of the fall now, on his forehead."

Margaret felt that the bad moment had passed.

"Tell me about your father, and all of you at home," she said. "Think! I have never even seen a picture of Uncle James! He is tall, of course; all the Montforts are tall."

"Miles tall," said Peggy; "with broad shoulders, and a big brown beard. So jolly, Pa is! He is out on the farm all day, you know, and in the evening he sits in the corner and smokes his pipe, and the boys tell him what they have been doing, and they talk crops and cattle and pigs by the hour together."

"The boys?" inquired Margaret. "Your brothers?"

Peggy nodded, and began to count on her fingers.

"Jim, George, Hugh, Max, and Peter, boys; Peggy, Jean, Bessie, Flora, and Doris, girls. Oh, dear! I wish they were all here!"

"Ten whole cousins!" cried Margaret. "How rich I feel! Now you must tell me all about them, Peggy. Is Jim the eldest?"

"Eldest and biggest!" replied Peggy, beginning on the frosted cake. "Jim is twenty-five, and taller than Pa,—six feet four in his shoes. He has charge of the stock, and spends most of his time on horseback. His horse is nearly as big as an elephant, and he rides splendidly. I think you would like Jim," she said shyly.

"I am sure I should!" said Margaret heartily. "Who comes next?"

"George," said Peggy. "George isn't very nice, I think; I don't believe you'd like him. He has been to college, you know, and he sneers and makes fun of the rest of us, and calls us countrified."

Margaret was sure that she should not like George, but she did not say so. "He's very clever," continued Peggy, "and Pa is very proud of him. I s'pose I might like him better if he didn't tease Hugh, but I can't stand that."

"Is Hugh your favourite brother?" Margaret asked softly.

"Of course. Hugh is the best of us all. He is lame. Jim and George were fighting one day, when he was a little baby, just beginning to walk; and somehow, one of them fell back against him and threw him downstairs. He hurt his back, and has been lame ever since. Hugh is like an angel, somehow. You never saw anybody like Hugh. He does things—well! Let me tell you this that he did. He never gets into rows, but the rest of us do, all the time. Jim and George are the worst, and when they are at it, you can hear them all over the house. Well, one day Hugh was sick upstairs, and they had an awful row. Pa was out, and Ma couldn't do anything with them; she never can. Hugh can generally stop them, but this time he couldn't go down, you see. I was sitting with him, and I saw him getting whiter and whiter. At last he said, 'Peggy, I want you—' and then he stopped and said, 'No, you are too big. Bring little Peter here!' I went and brought Peter, who was about four then. 'Petie,' said Hugh, 'take brother's crutch, and go downstairs, and give it to Brother Jim and Brother George. Say Hugh sent it.' And then he told me to help Petie down with the crutch, but not go into the room. I did peep in through the crack, though, and I saw Petie toddle in, dragging the crutch, and saw him lay it down between them, and say, 'Brudder Hugh send it to big brudders.' They stopped and never said another word, only Jim gave a kind of groan. Then he kissed Petie and told him to thank Brother Hugh; and he went out, and didn't come back for three days. He rides off when he feels bad, and stays away on the farm somewhere till he gets over it."

"And George?" asked Margaret.

"Oh! George just went into his room and sulked," said Peggy. "That's his way! I do declare, he's like—" Here she stopped suddenly, for a vision appeared in the doorway. Pale and scornful, with her great dark eyes full of cold mockery, Rita stood gazing at them both, her rose-coloured draperies floating around her.

"I am truly sorry," she said, "to interrupt this torrent of eloquence. I merely wish to say that I am going to bed. Good night, chère Marguerite! Senorita Calibana, je vous souhaite le bon soir! Continue, I pray you, your thrilling disclosures as long as my cousin's ears can contain them!" And with a mocking courtesy she swept away, leaving the other two girls with an indefinable sense of guilt and disgrace. Poor Peggy! She had been so happy, all her troubles forgotten, pouring out her artless recital of home affairs; but now her face darkened, and she looked sullen and unhappy again.

"Hateful thing!" she muttered. "I wish she was in Jericho!"

"Never mind, Peggy dear!" said Margaret as cheerfully as she could. "Rita is very tired, and has a headache. It has been delightful to hear about the brothers, and especially about Hugh; but I am sure we ought to go to bed too. You must be quite tired out, and I am getting sleepy myself."

She kissed her cousin affectionately, and arm in arm they went up the great staircase.

CHAPTER III

THE WHITE LADY OF FERNLEY

Margaret was waked the next morning by the cheerful and persistent song of a robin, which had perched on a twig just outside her window. She had gone to bed in a discouraged frame of mind, and dreamed that her two cousins had turned into lionesses, and were fighting together over her prostrate body; but with the morning light everything seemed to brighten, and the robin's song was a good omen.

"Thank you, Robin dear," she said aloud, as she brushed her long hair. "I dare say everything will go well after a while, but just now, Robin, I do assure you, things have a kittle look."

She was down first, as the night before; but Peggy soon appeared, rubbing her eyes and looking still half asleep.

Breakfast was ready, and Peggy, at sight of the omelette and muffins, was about to fling herself headlong into her chair; but Margaret held her back a moment.

"Elizabeth," she said, hesitating, "is Mrs. Cheriton—is she not here? I see you have put me at the head of the table again."

"Mrs. Cheriton seldom leaves her own rooms, miss," replied Elizabeth. "She asked me to say that she would be glad to see the young ladies after breakfast. And shall I call the other young lady, Miss Montfort?"

Before Margaret could reply, a clear voice was heard calling from above, in impatient tones:

"Elizabeth! somebody! come here this moment!"

Elizabeth obeyed the imperious summons, and as she reached the foot of the stairs, Rita's voice broke out again.

"Why has no coffee been brought to me? I never saw such carelessness. There is no bell in my room, either, and I have been calling till I am hoarse."

"I am very sorry, miss!" replied Elizabeth quietly. "We supposed you would come down to breakfast with the other young ladies. Shall I bring you a cup of tea now? There is no coffee in the house, as Mr. Montfort never drinks it."

"No coffee!" cried Rita. "I have come to a wilderness! Well—bring the tea! and have it strong, do you hear?" And the young Cuban swept back into her room, and shut the door with more vehemence than good breeding strictly allowed.

Margaret listened in distressed silence to this colloquy. Peggy giggled and chuckled. "Aha!" she said, "I'm so glad she didn't get the coffee. Greedy thing! Please hand me the muffins, Margaret. How small they are! The idea of her having her breakfast in bed!" and Peggy sniffed, and helped herself largely to marmalade.

"Perhaps her head aches still," said peace-loving Margaret.

"Don't believe a word of it!" cried Peggy. "She's used to being waited on by darkeys, and she thinks it will be just the same here. That's all!"

Margaret thought this was probably true, but she did not say so, preferring the safer remark that it was a delightful day.

"When you have finished your breakfast," she said, "we will go out into the garden. I can see a bit of it from here, and it looks lovely. Oh! I can just catch a glimpse of the swing. I wonder if it is the same old one. I love to swing, don't you?"

"I like shinning better!" said Peggy, putting half a muffin in her mouth. "Can you shin?"

"Shin! what—oh! up a tree, you mean. I'm afraid not."

"I can!" said Peggy triumphantly. "I can beat most of the boys at it, only Ma won't let me do it, on account of my clothes. Says I'm too old, too; bother! I'm not going to be a primmy, just because I am fifteen. How old are you, Margaret?"

"Seventeen; and as two years make a great difference, you know, Peggy, I shall put on all the airs of an elder sister. You know the Elder Sister's part,—

> "Good advice and counsel sage,
> And 'I never did so when I was your age!'"

"All right!" said Peggy. "I'll call you elder sister. Ma always says I ought to have had one, instead of being one."

"Well, first comes something that we must both do; that is, go and see Mrs. Cheriton; and if you will let me, dear, I am going to tie your necktie for you."

Peggy submitted meekly, while Margaret pulled the crumpled white tie round to the front, re-tied, patted, and poked it. Then her hair must be coaxed a little—or not so very little!—and then—

"What have you done to your frock, child? it is buttoned all crooked! Why, isn't there a looking-glass in your room?"

"Oh, yes!" said Peggy. "But I hate to look in the glass! There's sure to be something the matter, and I do despise fussing over clothes."

By this time Margaret had rebuttoned the dress, with a sigh over the fact that the buttons did not match it, and that one sleeve was put in wrong. Now she declared that they must go without more delay, and Elizabeth came to show them the way.

Peggy hung back, muttering that she never knew what to say to strangers; but Margaret took her hand firmly, and drew her along.

Perhaps Margaret may have felt a little nervous herself about this strange lady, who never left her rooms, and yet was to entertain and care for them, as her uncle's note had said. Both girls followed in silence, as Elizabeth led them through the hall, past a door, then down three steps and along a little passage to another door, at which she knocked.

"Come in!" said a pleasant voice. Elizabeth opened the door and motioned the girls to enter.

"The young ladies, ma'am!" she said; and then shut the door and went away.

The sudden change from the dark passage to the white room was dazzling. It was a small room, and it seemed to be all white: walls, floor (covered with a white India matting), furniture, and all. The strange lady sat in a great white armchair. She wore a gown of soft white cashmere, and her hair, and her cap, her hands, and her face, were all different shades of white, each softer than the other. Only her eyes were brown; and as she looked kindly at the girls and smiled, they thought they had never seen anything so beautiful in their lives.

"Why, children," she said; "do you think I am a ghost? Come here, dears, and let me look at you! I am real, I assure you." She laughed, the softest little laugh, hardly more than a rustle, and held out her hand. Margaret came forward at once, still dragging Peggy after her,—Peggy, whose eyes were so wide open, it looked as if she might never be able to shut them again.

Mrs. Cheriton took a hand of each, and looked earnestly from one to the other.

"How are you called?" she asked. "I know that you have the same name."

"We thought I had better be Margaret," was the timid reply from the girl who was able to speak, "and this is Peggy."

"I see!" said the old lady, putting her hand on Peggy's flaxen mane.

"You look like Peggy, little one! I used to call my sister Peggy. And where is the third Margaret?"

"She has not come down yet; she had a headache last night," said Margaret, losing all shyness before the kindly glance of those soft brown eyes. "She is called Rita, and she is very beautiful."

"That is pleasant!" said Mrs. Cheriton. "I like pretty people, when they are good as well. You are a Montfort, Margaret! You have the Montfort mouth, and chin; but this child must look like her mother." Peggy nodded, but could not yet find speech.

"And now," the old lady went on, "I am sure you are longing to know who I am, and why I live here by myself, like an old fairy godmother. Sit down, my dears, and be comfortable! Here, Margaret, the little rocking-chair is pleasant; Peggy, child, take the footstool! So! now you look more at home.

"Well, children, the truth is, I am very old. When my next birthday comes, I shall be ninety years old; a very great age, my dears! Your grandfather was my cousin; and when, five years ago, I was left alone in the world by the death of my dear only son, John Montfort, your uncle, like the good lad he is, found me out and brought me home with him to live. He is my godson, and I loved him very much when he was a little child; so now, when I am old and helpless, he makes return by loving me."

She paused to wipe her eyes; then went on.

"When one is nearly ninety years old, one does not care to move about much, even if one is perfectly well, as I am. John knew this (he knows a great deal), and he fitted up these pleasant rooms, in the warmest and quietest corner of the house, and here he put me, with my little maid, and my books, and my cat, and my parrot; and here I live, my dears, very cheerfully and happily. On pleasant days I go out in my garden, and sit under the trees. Look out of the window, girls, and see my green parlour. Is it not pretty?"

The girls knelt on the broad window-seat, and looked out. Before them was a square, grassy place, smooth and green as an emerald. The house enclosed it on two sides; the other two were screened by a hedge of Norway fir, twenty feet high, and solid as a wall. Over this the sunbeams poured in, flecking the green with gold. In one corner stood a laburnum-tree, covered with yellow blossoms; under a tall elm near by was a rustic seat.

"How do you like my kingdom?" asked the old lady, smiling at their eager faces.

"It is like a fairy place!" said Margaret. "You are quite sure you are real, Mrs. Cheriton?" They smiled at each other, feeling friends already.

"'Mrs. Cheriton' will never do, if we are to see each other every day, as I hope we are. How would you like to call me Aunt Faith?"

"Oh, the lovely name!" cried Margaret. "Thank you so much! Now we really belong to some one, and we shall not feel strange any more; shall we, Peggy?"

"I—s'pose not!" stammered Peggy. "I shall like it ever so much."

The girls sat a little longer, chatting and listening. Mrs. Cheriton told them of her parrot, who was old too, and who spoke Spanish and French, and did not like English; she showed them her books, many of which were bound in white vellum or parchment. "It is a fancy of John's," she said, "to have all my belongings white. I think he still remembers his Aunt Phoebe. Do you know about your Great-aunt Phoebe?"

The girls said no, and begged to hear, but Mrs. Cheriton said that must be for another time.

"I must not keep you too long," she said, "for I want you to come often. I will call Janet, and she shall show you the way through my green parlour to the garden. The Fernley garden is the pleasantest in the world, I think."

She touched the bell, and told the pretty rosy-cheeked maid who appeared to take the young ladies by the back way, and introduce them to Chiquito; and they took their leave regretfully, begging that they might come every day to the white chamber.

Chiquito's cage hung in the porch, and Chiquito was hanging in it upside down. He swore frightfully at the sight of strangers, and bit Peggy's finger when she tried to stroke him; but at a word from Janet he was quiet, and said, "Me gustan todas!" in a plaintive tone, with his head on one side.

"What does that mean?" asked Peggy. "He's horrid, isn't he?"

Janet's feeling were hurt. "He doesn't mean it!" she said. "And he always wants to be pleasant when he says that. Something out of a Spanish song, Mrs. Cheriton says it is, and means that he likes folks. You do like folks when they like you, don't you, poor Chico?"

"En general!" said the bird, cocking his yellow eye at Peggy. "Me gustan todas en general!"

"Well, I never!" said Peggy. "I think he's a witch, Margaret."

They went through a low door cut in the green wall, and found themselves in the great shady garden, a place of wonder and mystery. The trees and plants had been growing for two hundred years, ever since James Montfort had left the court of Charles II. in disgust, and come out to build his home and make his garden in the new country, where freedom waited for her children.

The great oaks and elms and chestnuts were green with moss and hoary with lichens, but the flower-beds lay out in broad sunshine, and here were no signs of age, only of careful tending and renewal. Margaret was enchanted with the flowers, for her home had been in a town, and she knew little of country joys. Peggy glanced carelessly at the geraniums and heliotropes, and told Margaret that she should see a field of poppies in bloom.

They came across the gardener, who straightened himself at sight of them, and greeted them with grave politeness. He was a tall, strongly made man, with, grizzled hair and bright, dark eyes.

"May we pick a few flowers?" asked Margaret in her pleasant way.

"Surely, miss; any, and all you like, except these beds of young slips here, which I am nursing carefully. I hope you will be often in the garden, young ladies!" and he saluted again, in military fashion, as the girls walked away.

"What a remarkable-looking man!" said Margaret. "I wonder if I can have seen him anywhere. There is something about his face—"

"Oh, there is the swing!" cried Peggy. "Come along, Margaret; I'll race you to that big chestnut-tree!" and away flew the two girls over the smooth green turf.

CHAPTER IV

CONFIDENCE

"What are you doing, très chère?" asked Rita, suddenly appearing at Margaret's door. "How is it you pass your time so cheerfully? how to live, in this deplorable solitude? You see me fading away, positively a shadow, in this hideous solitude!"

Margaret looked up cheerfully from her work.

"Come in, daughter of despair!" she said. And Rita came in and flung herself on the sofa with a tragic air.

"You are doing—what?" she demanded.

"I have rather a hopeless task, I fear," said Margaret. "Peggy's hat! She dropped it into the pond yesterday, and I am trying to smarten it up a little, poor thing! What do you advise, Rita? I am sure you have clever fingers, you embroider so beautifully."

"I should advise the fire," said Rita, looking with scorn at the battered hat. "Put it in now, this moment. It will burn well, and it can do nothing else decently."

"Ten miles from a shop," said Margaret, "and nothing else save her best hat. No, my lady, we cannot be so extravagant. If you will not help me, I must e'en do the best I can. I never could understand hats!" she added ruefully.

"Why do you do these things?" Rita asked, sitting up as suddenly as she had flung herself down. "Will you tell me why? I love you! I have told you twenty times of it; but I cannot understand why you do these things for that young monster. Will you tell me why?"

"In the first place, she is not a monster, and I will not have you say such things, Rita. In the second place, I am very fond of her; and in the third, I should try to help her all I could, even if I were not fond of her."

"Why?"

"Because it is a duty."

"Duty?" Rita laughed, and made a pretty little grimace. "English word, ugly and stupid word! I know not its meaning. You are fond of Calibana? Then I revere less your taste, that is all. Ah! what do you make there? That cannot be; it cuts the soul!"

She took the hat hastily from Margaret's hand. Had the latter been a little overclumsy on purpose? Certainly her dimple deepened a little as she relinquished the forlorn object. Rita held it on her finger and twirled it around.

"The fire is really the only place for it," she said again; "but if it must be preserved, do you not see that the only possible thing is to turn this ribbon? It was not wet through; the other side is fresh."

She still frowned at the hat, but her fingers began to move here and there, twisting and turning in a magical way. In five minutes the hat was a different object, and Margaret gave a little cry of pleasure.

"Rita, you are a dear! Why, it looks better than it did before the wetting, ever and ever so much better! Thank you, you clever creature! I shall bring all my hats to you for treatment, and I am sure Peggy will be so much obliged when I tell her—"

"If you dare!" cried Rita. "You will do nothing of the sort, I beg, ma cousine. What I have done, was done for you; I desire neither thanks nor any other thing from La Calibana. That she remain out of my sight when possible, that she hold her tongue when we must be together,—that is all I demand. Reasonable, I hope? If not—" She shrugged her shoulders and began to hum a love-song.

Margaret sighed. "If you could only see, my dear," she began gently, "how much happier we should all be, if you and Peggy could only make up your minds to make the best of it—"

"The best!" cried Rita, flashing into another mood, and coming to hover over her quiet cousin like a bird of paradise. "Do I not make the best? You are the best, Marguerite. I make all I can of you—except a milliner; never could I do that."

"Listen!" she added, dropping on the floor by Margaret's side. "You see me happy to-day, do you not? I do not frown or pout,—I can't see why I should not, when I feel black,—but to-day is a white day. And why? Can you guess?"

Margaret shook her head discreetly.

"I cannot do more than guess," she said, "but you seemed very much pleased with the letter that came this morning."

Rita flung her arms round her. "Aha!" she cried. "We perceive! We drop our dove's eyes; we look more demure than any mouse, but we perceive! Ah! Marguerite, behold me about to give you the strongest proof of my love: I confide in you."

She drew a bulky letter from her pocket. Margaret looked at it apprehensively, fearing she knew not what.

"From my friend," Rita explained, spreading the sheets of thin blue paper, crossed and recrossed, on her lap; "my Conchita, the other half of my soul. You shall hear part of it, Marguerite, but other parts are too sacred. She begins so beautifully: 'Mi alma'—but you have no Spanish yet; the pity, to turn it into cold English! 'My soul' has a foolish sound. 'Saint Rosalie, Saint Eulalie, and the blessed Saint Teresa, have you in their holy keeping! I live the life of a withered leaf without you; my soul flies like a mourning bird to your frozen North, where you are immured'—oh, it doesn't sound a bit right! I cannot read it in English." Indeed, Margaret thought it sounded too silly for her beloved language, but she said nothing, only giving a glance of sympathetic interest.

"She tells me of all they are doing," Rita went on. "All day they sit in the closed rooms, as the sun is too hot for going out; but in the evening they drive, and Conchita has been allowed to ride on horseback. Fancy, what bliss! Fernando was with her!"

Rita stopped suddenly, and Margaret, feeling that she must say something, echoed, "Fernando?"

"Her brother," said Rita, and she cast down her eyes. "Also a friend of mine,—a cousin on my mother's side; the handsomest person in Havana, the most enchanting, the most distinguished! He sends me messages,—no matter about those; but think of this: he is leaving Havana, he is coming to New York, he will be in this country! Marguerite! think of it!"

"What shall I think of it?" asked Margaret, raising her eyes to her cousin's; the gray eyes were cool and tranquil, but the dark ones were full of fire and light.

"Is he a friend of your father's, too, Rita?"

Rita's face darkened. "My father!" she cried impatiently. "My father is a knight of the middle ages; he demands the stiff behaviour of fifty in a youth of twenty-one. He, who has forgotten what youth is!" She was silent for a moment, but the shadow remained on her beautiful face.

"After all, it is no matter," she said, rising abruptly; "I was mistaken, Marguerite. The letter is for me alone; you would not care for it,—perhaps not understand it. You, too, have the cold Northern blood. Forget what I have said."

"Oh, but, my dear," cried Margaret, fearful of losing her slight hold on this creature of moods, "don't be so unkind! I want to know why they must sit in the house all day, and what they do from morning till night. I have always longed to know about the life you live at home. Be good now, wild bird, and perch again."

Rita wavered, but when Margaret laid her cool, firm hand on hers, she sank down again, though she still looked dissatisfied.

"We sit in the house," she said, "of course, in the heats,—what else could we do? Only at night is it possible to go out. No, we do not read much. It is too hot to read, and Cuban women do not care for books; oh, a romance now and then; but for great, horrible books like those you raffole about downstairs there,—" she shook her shoulders as if shaking off a heavy weight. "We sew a great deal, embroider, do lace-work like that you admired. Then at noon we sleep as long as possible, and in the evening we go out to walk, drive, ride. To walk in the orange-groves by moonlight,—ah! that is heaven! One night last month we slipped out, Conchita and I, and—you must never breathe this, Marguerite—and met my brother and Fernando beneath the great orange-tree in the south grove—"

"Your brother!" exclaimed Margaret. "You never told me you had a brother, Rita!"

"Hush! I have so much the habit of silence about him. He is with the army. My father is a Spaniard. Carlos and I are Cubans." Her eyes flashed, and she looked like the spirit of battle.

"My father will not hear him named!" she cried. "He would have Cuba continue a slave, she, who will be the queen and goddess of the sea when the war is over! Ah, Marguerite! my heart is on flame when I speak of my country. Well,—we met them there. They are both with the army, the insurgents, as the Spaniards call them. We walked up and down. The orange-blossoms were so sweet, the fragrance hung like clouds in the air. I had a lace mantilla over my head,—I will show it to you one day. We talked of Cuba libre, and they told us how they live there in the mountains. Ah! if a girl could fight, would I be here? No; a sword should be by my side, a plume in my hat, and I would be with Carlos and Fernando in the mountains. Well,—ah, the bad part is to come! Carlos had been wounded; his arm was in a sling. Folly, to make it of a white handkerchief! The señora—my father's wife—must have seen it shining among the trees; we know it must have been that, for we girls wore black dresses of purpose,—a woman thinks of what a man never dreams of. She called my father; he came out, raging. We had a fine scene. Burning words passed between my father and

Carlos. They vowed never to see each other more. They went, and Conchita and I go fainting, dying, into the house. Three days after comes my uncle's letter,—behold me here! Marguerite, this is my story. Preserve it in your bosom, it is a sacred confidence."

Margaret hardly knew whether she were in real life, or in a theatre. Rita's voice, though low, vibrated with passion; her eyes were liquid fire; her little hands clenched themselves, and she drew her breath in through her closed teeth with a savage sound. Then, suddenly, all was changed. She flung her arms apart, and burst into laughter.

"Your face!" she cried. "Marguerite, your face! what a study of horror! You, cool stream, flowing over white sands, you have never seen a rapid, how much less a torrent. You, do you know what life is? My faith, I think not! I frighten you, my cousin."

Margaret was indeed troubled as well as absorbed in all she had heard. What a volcano this girl was! What might she not do or say, in some moment of passion? This was all new to Margaret; her life had been so sheltered, a quiet stream indeed, till her father's death the year before. She had known few girls save her schoolmates, for the most part quiet, studious girls like herself. She had lived a great deal in books, and knew far more about Spain in the sixteenth century than Cuba in the nineteenth. What should she do? How should she learn to curb and help these two restless spirits, so different, yet both turning to her and flying in detestation from each other?

Pondering thus, she made no reply for a moment; but Rita was in no mood to endure silence.

"Statue!" she cried. "Thing of marble! I pour out my soul to you, and you have no words for me! And we have been here a week, a mortal, suffering week, and I know nothing of your life, your thought. Tell me, you, how you have lived, before you came here. I frighten you, I see it; try now if you can tame me."

She laughed again, and shook all her pretty ribbons and frills.

Every day she dressed as if for a fête, and took a mournful pleasure in reflecting how her toilets were all wasted.

"How did I live?" said Margaret vaguely. "Oh, very quietly, Rita. So quietly, I don't think you would care to hear about my days."

"I burn to hear!" cried Rita. "I perish! Continue, Marguerite."

"I lived with my dear father." Margaret spoke slowly and reluctantly. Her memories were so precious, she could not bear to drag them out, and expose them to curious, perhaps unloving, eyes.

"Our house was in Blankton, a tiny little house, just big enough for Father and me; my mother died, you know, a good many years ago, and Father and I have been always together. He wrote a great deal,—historical work,—and I helped him, and wrote for him, and read with him. Then—oh, I went to school, of course, and we walked every afternoon, and in the evening Father read aloud while I worked, and I played and sang for him. You see, Rita, there really is not much to tell."

Not much! yet in the telling, the girl felt her heart beat high and painfully, and the sobs rise in her throat, as the dear, happy, peaceful days came back to her; the blessed home life, the love which hedged her in so that no rough wind should blow on her, the wise, kindly, loving companionship of him who had been father and mother both to her. The tears came to her eyes, and she was silent, feeling that she could not speak for the moment. Rita was thoughtful, too, and when she spoke again, it was in a softened tone.

"I can picture it!" she said. "It is a picture without colour; I could not have borne such a life; but for you, Marguerite, so tranquil, demanding so little, with peace in your soul, it must have been sweet. And now,—after this summer here, only not horrible because in it I learn to know my dear Marguerite,—after this summer, what do you do? what is your life?"

"I hope to get a position as teacher," said Margaret. "Then, when I have earned something, I shall go to the Library School, and learn to be a librarian; that has been my dream for a long time."

"Your nightmare!" cried Rita. "What dreadful things even to think about, Marguerite! But it shall not be; never, I tell you! You shall come back with me to Cuba, and be my sister. I have money—oceans, I believe; more than I can spend, try as I will. You shall live with me; we will buy a plantation, orange-groves, sugar-cane,—you shall study cultivation, I will ride about the plantation—"

"By moonlight?" asked Marguerite mischievously.

"Always by moonlight!" cried Rita. "It shall be always moonlight! Carlos shall be our intendant, and Fernando—"

"I think Fernando would much better stay in the mountains!" said Margaret decidedly.

CHAPTER V

THE PEAT-BOG

It was a great relief to Margaret to carry her perplexities to Aunt Faith and talk them over. Mrs. Cheriton's mind and sympathies were as quick and alert as if she were still a young woman, instead of being near the rounding of the completed century. She listened with kindly interest, and her wise and tender words cleared away many of the cobwebs of anxiety that beset Margaret's sky.

"Let patience have her perfect work!" she was fond of saying. "Neither of these children is to be led by precept, I think. Make your own ways, ways of pleasantness as well as paths of peace, and soon or late they will fall into them. You cannot expect to do much in a week, or two weeks, or three weeks. Or it may be," she would add, "that you are not to do it after all; it may be that other things and persons will be called in. The ordering is wise, but we cannot often understand it, for it is written in cipher. Do you only the best you can, my child, and keep your own head steady, and you will find the others settling into harness before long."

"It distresses me," Margaret said, "to have Rita so rude to the servants. I cannot speak to her about that, I suppose; but it is really too bad. Elizabeth is so sensible, I am sure she understands how it all is; but—well, the gardener, Aunt Faith! John Strong! Why, any one can see that he is an uncommon man; not the least an ordinary labouring man. Do you know how much he knows?"

Mrs. Cheriton nodded. "John Strong is a very remarkable man," she said; "you are right there, Margaret. And Rita is uncivil to him? Do you know, I should not trouble myself about that if I were you. If Elizabeth can understand that Rita has been brought up without learning any respect for the dignity of labour, John Strong will understand it twice as well, for he has more than twice the intelligence."

"Thank you, Aunt Faith! You are so comforting! He—he has been here a long time, has he not? I should think my uncle must have great confidence in him; and he has such beautiful manners!"

"His manners," said Mrs. Cheriton emphatically, "are perfect." Then she said, changing the subject rather hastily, "And where are the two other girls to-day, my dear? They do not incline to come to me often, I perceive. It is not strange; many very young people dislike the sight of extreme age; you have been taught differently, my dear,—Roger Montfort was always a thoughtful, sensible lad, like John. No, I do not blame them in the least for keeping away, but I like to know what they are doing."

"I—I don't really know, just now," and Margaret hung her head a little; "Peggy wanted me to go to walk with her an hour or so ago, but I was just reading a book that Papa had always told me about,—'The Fool of Quality,' you know it?—and I did not want to leave it. I ought to have gone; I will go now, and see where they both are. Dear Aunt Faith, thank you so much for letting me come and talk to you; you can't think what a relief it is when I am puzzled."

The old lady's sweet smile lingered like a benediction with Margaret, as she went back to the main house, carefully closing the door that shut off the white rooms. Surely she had been selfish to stay indoors with a book, instead of going out with her cousin; but oh, the book understood her so much better, and was so much more companionable! Now, however, she would be good, and would go and see what both the cousins were doing. They were not together, of course; Rita was very likely asleep at this hour; but Peggy, what had Peggy been doing?

What had Peggy been doing?

She had sauntered out rather disconsolately, on Margaret's refusing to accompany her. She was so used to being one of a large, shouting, struggling family, that she felt, perhaps more than any of the three girls, the retirement and quiet of Fernley. She wanted to run and scream and make a noise, but there was no fun in doing it alone. If Jean were only here!

She went through the garden, and found some consolation in a talk with John Strong, who, always the pink of courtesy, leaned on his hoe, and told her many valuable things concerning the late planting. Her questions were shrewd and intelligent, for Peggy had not lived on a farm for nothing, and she already knew more about the possibilities of Fernley than Margaret or Rita would learn in a year.

"Where shall I go for a walk?" she asked, when John Strong showed signs of thinking about his work again. "I hate to go alone, but no one would come with me. I have been over the hill and into the oak woods. What is another nice way to go, where there will be strawberries?"

John Strong considered. "About two miles from here, miss, you'll find a very pretty strawberry patch. Go through the oak woods and along beside the bog; but be careful not to step into the bog itself, for it is a treacherous bit."

"What kind of a bog? Why don't you drain it?" asked Peggy.

"It is a peat-bog," returned the gardener. "It would be a very costly matter to drain it, but I believe Mr. Montfort is thinking of it, miss. A short way beyond the woods you'll come upon the strawberry meadow; it is the best I know of hereabouts. Good morning, miss."

Off went Peggy, swinging her hat by the ribbon, a loop of which was coming off, and thinking of home and of Jean, her most intimate sister. She loved Margaret dearly already, but one had always to be on one's good behaviour with her, she was so good herself. Oh, how delightful it would be to have Jean here, and to have a race through the woods, and then a good, jolly romp, and perhaps a "spat," before they settled down to the business of strawberry-picking! She could have spats enough with that horrid, spiteful Cuban girl, but there was no fun in those; just cold, sneering hatefulness. Thinking of her cousin Rita, Peggy gave her hat a twist and a fling, and sent it flying across the green meadow on which she was now entering.

"There!" she said, "I just wish that was you, Miss Rita,—I do! I wouldn't help you up, either."

Then, rather ashamed of her outburst, she went to pick up the hat again; but, setting foot on the edge of the green meadow, she drew it back hastily.

"Aha!" said Peggy. "The peat-bog! Now I've been and gone and done it!"

She whistled, a long, clear whistle that would have done credit to any one of her brothers, and gazed ruefully at the hat, which lay out of reach, resting quietly on the smooth emerald velvet of the quaking bog.

"Oh, bother! Now I suppose I shall have to fish the old thing out. It will never look fit to be seen again, and Margaret retrimmed it only the other day. Well, here goes!"

Looking about carefully, Peggy pulled a long bulrush from a clump that grew at the side of the bog. Then she walked along the edge, skirting with care the deceitful green that looked so fair and lovely, till she came to where a slender birch hung its long drooping branches out over the bog. Clinging to one of these branches, Peggy leaned forward as far as she dared, and began to angle for her hat. "He rises well," she muttered, "but he doesn't bite worth a cent."

Twice she succeeded in working the end of the bulrush through the loop of ribbon that perked cheerfully on the top of the hat; twice the loop slipped off as she raised it, and the hat dropped back. The third time, however, was successful, and the skilful angler had the satisfaction of drawing the hat toward her, and finally rescuing it from its perilous position. Not all of it, however; the flower, the yellow rose, once Peggy's pride and joy, had become loosened during the various unaccustomed motions of its parent hat, and now lay, lonely and lovely, a golden spot on the bright green grass.

Peggy fished again, but this time in vain; and finally she was obliged to give it up, and go off flowerless in search of her strawberries.

Meanwhile, Margaret had been searching high and low for Peggy. John Strong could have told her where she was, but he had gone to a distant part of the farm, and no one had seen the two talking together.

"A search for Calibana?" said Rita, when her cousin inquired for the wanderer. "My faith, why? If she can remain hidden for a time, Marguerite, consider the boon it would be!"

But Margaret turned from her impatiently, seeing which, Rita was jealous, and said, "I had hoped you would take a walk with me, ma cousine. I perish for air! I cannot go alone through these places,—I might meet a dog."

Margaret could not help laughing.

"I think you might," she said. "And what then?"

"I should die!" said Rita simply. Then, linking her arm in her cousin's with her most caressing gesture, she said, "Come with me, alma mia. We walk,—very likely we find La Calibana on our way. She cannot have strayed far, it is too near dinner-time; and she has a clock inside her; you know it well, Marguerite."

Margaret could not refuse the offered company, and they set out in the same direction that Peggy had taken. Margaret had been in the oak woods several times with Peggy, and thought she might very likely find her there; but no one answered her call; only the trees rustled, and the hermit-thrush called in answer, deep in some thicket far away. Presently, as they walked, there shot through the dark oak branches a sunny gleam, a flash of green and gold. They pressed forward, and in another moment stood on the edge of the quaking bog.

But they had not been warned; neither had they Peggy's practised eye, which would have told her even without the warning that this was no safe place.

"Oh, what a lovely meadow!" cried Margaret. "I always wondered what lay beyond these woods, but have never come so far before. Shall we cross it, Rita? or does it look a little damp, do you think?"

"It may be damp," said Rita indifferently. "I care not for damp, très chère. Let us cross, by all means. And look! see the golden flower; what can it be?"

"I don't know, I am sure!" said Margaret, gazing innocently at the yellow muslin rose which had been under her hands only the day before. "It looks—I don't know what it looks like, Rita. But I am afraid the grass is very wet. Don't you see the wet shining through?"

"Pouf!" said Rita. "Wait thou here, faint heart, while I bring the flower; that, at least, I must do, even if we go no further."

She stepped over the grass so lightly and quickly that she had gone some steps before her feet began to sink in the black, oozy bog. Margaret saw the water bubbling up behind her, and cried to her in alarm to come back; and Rita, finding the earth plucking at her feet, turned willingly toward the solid ground; but return was impossible. She tried to lift her feet, but the bog held them fast, and with the effort, she felt herself sinking, slowly but surely.

"Ah," she cried, "it is bad ground! It is a pit, Marguerite! Do not move, do not come near me! Run and get help!" For Margaret was already stepping forward with outstretched hands.

"Stop where you are!" cried Rita imperiously. "Do you not see that if you come in, we are both lost? I tell you there is no ground here, no bottom! I sink, I feel it sucking me down, down! Ah, Madre! go, Marguerite, fly for help!"

Poor Margaret turned in distraction. Whither should she fly? They were more than a mile from home. How could she leave her cousin in this dreadful plight? Before help could come, she might be lost indeed, drawn bodily under by the treacherous ooze. She turned away, but came running back suddenly, for she heard a sound coming from the opposite direction, a cheerful whistle.

"Oh, Rita!" she cried; "help is near. I hear some one whistling, a boy or a man. Oh, help! help! Come this way, please!"

The whistle changed to a cry of surprise, uttered in a familiar voice. The next minute, Peggy came running through the wood, her hands and face red with strawberry juice.

Margaret could only gasp, and point to Rita, for her heart seemed to die within her when she saw that the newcomer was only a girl like herself,—only poor, awkward Peggy.

They were no better off than before, save that now one could go for help, while the other could stay to cheer poor Rita. Rita was now deadly white; she had ceased to call. The black ooze had crept to her knees, and she no longer made any effort to extricate herself. Margaret was turning to run again, but Peggy stopped her. "Stand still!" she said. "I'll get her out."

Ah, poor, awkward, ill-dressed Peggy, your hour has come now! Not for nothing were you brought up on a prairie, your eyes trained to quickness, your arms strong as steel, your wits ever on the alert where there is danger! Poor Peggy, this is your hour, and the haughty beauty and the gentle student must own you their superior.

Peggy cast a keen glance around; she was looking for something. Spying a stout stake that had been broken off and was lying on the ground, she caught it up, and the next moment had thrown herself flat on her face. Lying flat, she began slowly and cautiously to wriggle out across the surface of the quaking bog. The black water seethed and bubbled under her; but her weight, evenly distributed, did not bear on any one spot heavily enough to press her down. Slowly, carefully, she worked her way out, while the other girls held their breath and dared not speak. Once, indeed, Rita moaned, and cried, "No, no, one is enough! Go back! I cannot let you come!"

But Margaret had seen that in Peggy's eyes and mien which kept her silent. She stood trembling, with clasped hands, praying for both. She could do no more.

"Lie down now, Rita!" Peggy commanded. "Lie flat, just as I am! Stretch out your arms,—so! Now, catch hold!"

Rita obeyed to the point. It was terrible to lie down in that awful black slough that was to be her grave, perhaps, but she obeyed without a word. Stretching her arms as far as they would go, she touched the end of the stake,—touched, grasped, held fast; and now Peggy, still holding fast to her end, began to wriggle back, slowly, cautiously, moving by inches.

"Kneel down on the edge, Margaret!" she said; "don't come over, but reach out and give us a haul in when you can touch. It's getting pretty deep here!"

Margaret knelt and reached out her arms; could she touch them? Peggy was sinking now, but she still moved backward, dragging Rita with her; they were close by,—she had hold of Peggy's skirt. The stout gathers held,—which was a miracle, Peggy said afterward,—and the next moment all three girls were sitting on the safe, dry ground, crying and holding each other tight.

CHAPTER VI

THE FAMILY CHEST

Little was said on the homeward walk. Rita walked between her two cousins, holding fast a hand of each. She seemed hardly conscious of their presence, however; she sobbed occasionally, dry, tearless sobs, and murmured Spanish words to herself. Margaret caught the word "Madre!" repeated over and over, and pressed her cousin's hand, and spoke soothing words; but Rita did not heed her. Peggy walked quickly, head in air, cheeks glowing, and eyes shining. All the awkwardness, the hanging head and furtive air, was gone, and Margaret looked at her in wonder and admiration. But both girls were a piteous sight as regarded their clothes. From head to foot they dripped with black mud, thick and slimy. Peggy's dress gave no hint of the original colour in the entire front, and Rita's was little better.

Their very faces were bedabbled with black, and they left a black trail behind them on the grass. In this guise they met the astonished gaze of John Strong as he passed through the garden on his way to the seed-house. He came hurrying toward them with anxious looks.

"My dear children," he cried, "what has happened?" Then, in a different tone, "I beg your pardon, young ladies! I was startled at seeing you,—there has been some accident?"

But Rita was herself again now in an instant. Her eyes blazed with angry pride.

"Keep your place, John Strong!" she said haughtily. "When we address you, it will be time for you to speak to us." She swept past him into the house, her superb bearing presenting a singular contrast to her attire; and Peggy followed her, already beginning to giggle and look foolish again. But Margaret lingered, distressed and mortified.

"Oh, John," she said, "there has been an accident! You will understand,—Miss Rita got into that terrible bog, and might have been drowned there before my eyes, if Miss Peggy had not come by, and drawn her out so cleverly." And she told him the whole story, dwelling warmly upon Peggy's courage and presence of mind, and blaming herself for not having perceived the danger in time.

"It is I who am to blame, Miss Margaret!" said John Strong. "Very, very much to blame. Every one about here knows that peat-bog, and avoids it; I had warned Miss Peggy, but did not think of your going so far in that direction. I am very much to blame."

He seemed so much disturbed that Margaret tried to speak more lightly, though she was still pale and trembling; but the gardener kindly begged her to go in and rest, and she was glad enough to go.

John Strong stood looking after her a moment.

"I ought to be shot!" he said to himself. "And that is the lassie for me! Good stuff in both the others, as I supposed, but this is the one for me." And shaking his head, he went slowly on his way.

Margaret went straight to Peggy's room, but found it empty, and passing by Rita's found the door shut, and heard voices within. She paused a moment, wondering. Should she go in? No; she remembered Mrs. Cheriton's words, "It may be that you are not to do it, after all," and she went into her own room and shut the door.

It might have been half an hour after that she heard a whispering in the hall outside, and then a knock at her door. She ran to open it, and stood amazed. There was Peggy, blushing and smiling, looking as pleased as a little child, arrayed in the rose-coloured tea-gown whose existence she had endangered on the night of her arrival; and there beside her, holding her hand, was Rita, in pale blue and swansdown,—Rita, also smiling, but with the mockery for once gone from eyes and mouth, and with traces of tears on her beautiful face. She now led Peggy forward, and presented her formally to Margaret, with a sweeping courtesy.

"Miss Montfort," she began, "this is my sister. I desire for her the honour and privilege of your distinguished acquaintance. She kisses your hands and feet, as do I myself."

Then suddenly she threw herself upon Margaret's neck, still holding Peggy's hand, so that all three were wrapped in one embrace.

"Marguerite," she cried, "behold this child! I have been a brute to her, you know it well—" and Margaret certainly did. "A brute, a devil-fish, what you will! and she—she has saved my life! You saw it, you heard it; another moment, and I should have gone—" she shuddered. "I cannot speak of it. But now, Marguerite, hear me swear!"

"Oh my!" ejaculated Peggy, in some alarm.

"Hear me swear!" repeated Rita passionately; "from this moment Peggy is my sister. You are not jealous, no? You are also my own soul, but you are sufficient to yourself; what do you need, piece of Northern perfection that you are? Peggy needs me; I take her, I care for her, I form her! so shall it be!" And once more she embraced both cousins warmly.

Margaret's eyes filled with happy tears.

"Dear Peggy! Dear Rita!" was all she could say at first, as she returned their embraces. Then she made them come in and sit down, and looked from one to the other. "It is so good!" she cried. "Oh, so good! You can't imagine, girls, how I have longed for this! It did seem so dreadful that you should not have the pleasure of each other—but we will not speak of that any more! No! and we will bless the black bog for bringing you together."

But Rita shuddered again, and begged that she might never hear of the bog again.

"Do you observe Peggy's hair?" she asked. "What do you think of it?"

The fair hair was brought smoothly up over the well-shaped head, and wound in a pretty, fluffy Psyche knot. The effect was charming in one way, but—

"It makes her look too grown-up," Margaret protested. "It is very pretty, but I want her to be a little girl as long as she can. You don't want to be a young lady yet, do you, Peggy?"

"Oh, no!" cried Peggy. "Indeed I don't! But Rita thought—"

"Rita thought!" cried that young lady, nodding her head sagely. "Rita thought wrong, as usual, and Margaret thought right. It is too old; but what of that? We will try another style. Ten, twenty ways of dressing hair I know. Often and often Conchita and I have spent a whole day dressing each other's hair, trying this effect, that effect. Ah, the superb hair that Conchita has; it sweeps the floor,—and soft—ah, as a bat's wool!"

A few hours ago, Peggy would have sniffed scornfully at all this; but now she listened with interest, and something of awe, as her beautiful cousin discoursed of braids and puffs, and told of the extraordinary effect that might sometimes be produced by a single small curl set at the proper curve of the neck. It sounded pretty frivolous, to be sure, but then, Rita looked so earnest and so lovely, and it was so new and delightful to be addressed by her as an equal,—and a beloved equal at that; Peggy's little head was in evident danger of being turned by the new position of affairs.

Margaret, feeling that there were limits, even to the subject of hairdressing, presently proposed a visit to Aunt Faith, and for once neither cousin made any objection. Peggy was mortally afraid of the white old lady, and Rita said frankly that she did not like old people, and saw no reason why she should put herself out, simply because her uncle, whom she had never seen, had chosen to saddle himself with the burden of a centenarian. But to-day, Rita was shaken and softened out of all her waywardness, and she readily admitted the propriety of telling Mrs. Cheriton what had happened.

Aunt Faith listened with deep interest, and was as shocked and distressed as heart could desire. The peat-bog, she told them, did not belong to their uncle; he had in vain tried to buy the land, in order that he might drain or fence it, but the proprietor refused to sell it. There was a terrible story, she said, of a man's being lost there, many years ago; it was a dreadful place.

Then, seeing Rita shudder again, she changed the subject, and spoke of the charming contrast of the pale blue and rose-colour, in the two girls' dresses. "The pink suits you well, little Peggy," she said. "I have not seen you in a delicate colour before."

"This isn't mine," said honest Peggy; "it is Rita's—" but Rita laid her hand over her mouth.

"It is hers!" she said; "a nothing! a tea-gown of last year! One is ashamed to offer such a thing, not fit to scour floors in—"

"Certainly not!" said Mrs. Cheriton, laughing.

"Ah, Rita! you have the Spanish ways, I see. I have heard nothing of that sort since I was in Spain sixty years ago."

"What, you have been in Spain!" cried Rita, with animation. "Ah, I did not know! Please tell us about it."

"Another time. You would like to hear, I think, about the winter I spent in Granada, close by the Alhambra. But now I have something else to say. Your pretty dresses remind me that there is a chest of old gowns here that it might interest you to look over. Some of them are quite old, two hundred years or more."

Then, while the girls uttered cries of delight, she called Janet and bade her open the cedar chest in the next room.

"This way, my dears!" and she led the way into a bedroom, as white and fresh and dainty as the sitting-room. Janet was already on her knees before a deep chest, quaintly carved, and clamped with brass. Now, at her mistress's request, she began to lift out the contents.

"Oh! oh! oh!" cried the three girls, positively squeaking with rapture and wonderment. The old lady looked from them to the dresses with a pleased smile. "They are handsome!" she said.

And they were! They must have been stately dames indeed, the Montfort ladies who wore these splendid clothes! Here was a crimson damask, so heavily embroidered in silver that it stood alone when Janet set it up on the floor; here, again, a velvet, somewhat rubbed by long lying in the chest, but of so rich and glowing a purple that only a queen could have found it becoming. Here were satins that gleamed like falling water; one, of the faint, moonlight tint that we call aqua-marine, another with a rosy glow like a reflected sunset. And the peach-coloured silk! and the blue and silver brocade! and the amber velvet!

Before the bottom of the chest was reached, the girls were silent, having exhausted their stock of words.

At last Margaret cried, "Who were these people, Aunt Faith? Were they princesses, or runaway Indian begums, or what? They certainly cannot have been simple gentlewomen!"

Mrs. Cheriton laughed her soft, rustling laugh.

"It is a curious old Montfort custom," she said; "it has come down through many generations, I believe. The women have had the habit of keeping the handsomest gown they had, or one connected with some special great event, and laying it in this old chest. Some of them are wedding-gowns,—those two satins, for example, and that white brocade with the tiny rosebuds,—that was your Grandmother Montfort's wedding-gown, my dears, and she looked like a rose in it; I was bridesmaid at her wedding. But others,—ah! hand me the blue and silver brocade, Janet! Yes, here is an inscription that will, I think, amuse you, my children. This was my own mother's contribution to the family chest."

She beckoned the girls to look, and they bent eagerly forward. Under the rich lace in the neck of the splendid brocade, a piece of paper was neatly stitched, and on the paper was written: "This

Gown was worne at Madam Washington's Ball. I danced with Gen. Washington, the Court Minuet, and he praised my dancing. Afterwards the Gen. spilled Wine uppon the Front Peece, but I put French Chalks to it, and now the Spotte may hardly be Seen."

"Oh," sighed Margaret, "how enchanting! how perfectly delightful! Are they all marked, Aunt Faith?"

"Not all, but a good many of them. See! Here is something on this sea-green cloak; notice the sleeves, Rita: they are something in the Spanish style, as it was in my youth. Let us see what is written here, for I forget."

They bent over the yellow writing; in this case it was pinned on the hanging sleeve, and read as follows: "This Cloak, with the flowered satin Gown, was worn by me, Henrietta Montfort, the last time I went to a worldly Assemblage. I lay them away, having entered upon a Life of Retirement and Meditation since the Death of my deere Husband. Mem. The Cloake was lined with Sabels, which I have removed, lest Moth and Rust do corrupt, and have made them into Muffs for the Poor."

"I believe she became a great saint," said Mrs. Cheriton, "and a very severe one. I have heard that in the coldest winter weather she would not let her servants build fires on Sunday because she did not consider it a necessary work. There is a story that one bitter cold Sunday some one came to call, and found the whole family in bed, servants and all, trying to keep warm. I know they never had any warm victuals on that day."

"How pleasant to live now," said Margaret, "instead of then! Aren't you glad, girls?"

"My faith!" said Rita, "I would have made a fire with the house, and burned her in it; then I should have been warm. But what is this, Aunt Faith? If I am truly to call you so, yes? What horror is this? Look at the beautiful satin, all destroyed! Cut!—it is cut with knives, Marguerite! Look!"

Janet held up a white satin gown, of quaint and graceful fashion. Sure enough, it was cut and slashed in every direction, the sleeves hanging in ribbons, the skirt slit and gashed down its entire length. Mrs. Cheriton shook her head in answer to the girls' looks of amazement and inquiry.

"I am sorry you saw that, Rita!" she said. "It recalls a sad story, which might better be forgotten. However—well, that gown belonged to my poor Aunt Penelope. She was a beautiful girl, but headstrong, and she married, against her parents' wishes, a handsome, good-for-nothing man, who made her desperately unhappy, and finally left her. She lost her mind, poor soul, from sorrow and suffering. When her father brought her home to Fernley, she took this, her wedding-gown, and cut it up in this strange fashion that you see, and laid it so in the chest; as a warning, she told her mother. She died very soon after her return; poor Aunt Penelope!"

She signed to Janet to lay the tattered gown back; and it seemed to the girls as if the poor lady herself were being laid back in her coffin to rest after her troubled life.

"Does—does she walk?" asked Peggy, in an awestruck voice.

"Walk?" repeated Mrs. Cheriton. "I don't—oh, yes! her ghost, you mean, Peggy? No, my dear. I fancy she was too tired to think of anything but resting. There is only one Montfort ghost that I ever heard of, and that one is not a woman's."

"Oh, tell us! Tell us, please!" cried all three girls eagerly. "A real ghost? How thrilling!"

"I did not say it was a real ghost, you impetuous children. I do not believe in ghosts myself, and I never saw this one. But people used to think that the spirit of Hugo Montfort haunted one of the rooms. He died suddenly, in great trouble about some family papers that had been lost, and the family tradition is that he comes back from time to time to hunt once more through desks and drawers, in hope of finding them. He has never done so, I believe; but then, he has never been here since I came to Fernley. Your Uncle John is no ghost-lover, any more than I am, and I fear poor Hugo may feel the lack of sympathy. And now," she added, "this is positively enough of old-time gossip. I do not know when I have talked so much, children; you make me young and frivolous once more."

"Oh," cried Peggy, who had listened open-mouthed to the last tale; "but just tell us what he looks like, when any one does see him. I have wanted all my life to be where there was a ghost. Is he—is he in white?"

"Oh, dear, no! Hugo Montfort is no hobgoblin ghost in a white sheet, with a pumpkin head! He was a very elegant gentleman in his time, and I believe his favorite wear is black velvet. By the way, his portrait is in the long gallery upstairs. Have you been there, my dears? There are some curious old portraits. And there is the garret; you have surely visited the garret?"

But the girls had not, they confessed. There had been so much to do, the days had gone so rapidly. Margaret alone realised, and she perhaps for the first time, how little they had really seen of the house itself. There was so much to see out of doors, and when indoors she was always drawn irresistibly to the library and its entrancing folios and quartos. Peggy had, one rainy day, proposed to "see if there wasn't a garret or some place where they could have some fun." But Margaret, as she now remembered with a pang, had just discovered the "Hakluyt Chronicles," and was conscious of nothing in the world save the volume before her, and the longing wish for her father to enjoy it with her.

"We will go this very afternoon!" she cried, with animation. "Is it unlocked? May we roam about wherever we like, Aunt Faith? It sounds like Bluebeard! Are there no doors that we may not open?"

"None among those that you will see there," said Mrs. Cheriton. And Margaret fancied that she looked grave for a moment. "You will find more trunks there," she added quickly, "full of old trumpery, less valuable than these dresses, and which you may like to amuse yourselves with. Here are the keys of some of them—the wig trunk, the military trunk; yes, I think you may be sure of an afternoon's amusement if you are as fond of dressing up as I was at your age. Now we must say good-bye, my dear children; Janet is shaking her head at me, and it is true that I must not talk too long."

She kissed them all affectionately, and they sped away, Margaret only lingering to look back with one parting glance at the beautiful old figure in its white chair.

"The garret! the garret!" cried Rita. "Hurrah!" shouted Peggy. And they flew up the stairs like swallows.

CHAPTER VII

THE GARRET

On the wide landing of the second story, the girls paused to draw breath and look about them. The long gallery ran around three sides of the house, with the stairs forming the fourth. It was hung with pictures, save where two or three doors broke the wall-space. Singular pictures they were, mostly family portraits, it was evident. Some of them were very good, though the gems of the collection, the Copleys and Stuarts, and the precious Sir Joshua Reynolds, were in the drawing-rooms below. The girls ran from one to the other, and great was their delight to recognise here and there one of the very gowns they had been admiring in the Family Chest.

"Here is Henrietta Montfort, in the sea-green cloak!" cried Margaret. "Look, girls, what a haughty, disagreeable face; I don't wonder her family trembled before her."

"And here—oh, here is Hugo!" cried Peggy; "black velvet, she said. Look here, Margaret!"

The portrait was that of a man in middle life, handsomely dressed in black velvet, with hat and ruff. His face was sad, but the bright, dark eyes looked intelligently at the girls, and the whole face had a familiar look.

"He has a look of Papa," said Margaret softly; "it is a weaker face, but there is a strong resemblance."

"I think he looks like John Strong," said Peggy decidedly.

"My dear Peggy," said Rita, "I must pray that you will take less notice of our uncle's gardener. What does it matter to you how he looks? I ask you. Now that you are my sister I must teach you to forget this habit of speaking to servants as if they were your equals.

I overheard you the other day conversing—absolutely conversing—with this man. Dear child, it is wholly unsuitable. I tell you, and I know."

Margaret, who loved peace almost too well, was tempted to let this pass, but her conscience shouted at her, and she spoke.

"I am sorry to have you regard John Strong as an ignorant or inferior person, Rita," she said gently, knowing that she seemed priggish, but encouraged by Peggy's confused and abashed look.

"I think that if you were to talk with him a little yourself, you would feel differently. He is a very superior man, and Uncle John has the highest opinion of him; Aunt Faith has told me so."

Rita shrugged her shoulders. "Really, très chère," she said, "this is a case in which it is not necessary, believe me, to go back a hundred years. We hear about the manners of the vieille école; my faith, the school may become too old!"

"Rita!" cried Margaret indignantly. "How can you?"

Rita only shrugged her shoulders; her eyes shone with the very spirit of wilfulness.

"Ma cousine," she said, "it is a thousand pities that you cannot come to Havana with me.

The quality of being always virtuous—it is abhorrent, très chère; correct it, if possible. And the garret cries out for us!" she said, turning away, with the straight line between her eyes that meant mischief, as Margaret had already learned. She turned to Peggy, who stood in some alarm, not knowing whether the old friend or the new should claim her allegiance.

"Allons!" she cried. "The door, Peggy! which door will take us to this place of joy? this one? Hein! it is locked; it will not open."

"That must be Uncle John's room," said Peggy. "It is always locked.

I—I have tried it two or three times." And she stole a guilty glance, which made the two older girls laugh outright.

"Fatima!" said Margaret, trying to speak lightly, though her heart still burned from Rita's insolent words. "Peggy, it is a dangerous thing to try doors in a house like Fernley."

"Oh, I dare say it is only a linen closet," said Peggy. "I shouldn't have cared, only it is provoking not to be able to see what is in there. But this is the garret door, this way. I went up part way once, but it seemed so big and spooky, I didn't want to go all the way alone."

It was a big place, indeed, this garret! The girls looked about them in wonder, as soon as their eyes grew accustomed to the dim light that came from the small gable windows. The corners were black and deep,—miles deep, poor Peggy thought, as she peered into them. Old furniture lay about, broken chairs and gouty-legged tables. In one corner a huge chest of drawers loomed, with round, hunched shoulders, as if it were leaning forward to watch them; in another—oh, mercy! what was that?

The three caught sight at once of an object so terrifying that Rita and Peggy both shrieked aloud, and turned to flee; but Margaret held them back.

"Girls," she said, and her voice trembled a little, whether from laughter or fear; "wait! It—it can't be what it looks like, you know! It must—" She advanced cautiously a few steps, and began to laugh. It certainly had looked at first like the figure of a man hanging from the rafters; it proved to be only an innocent suit of clothes, dangling its legs in a helpless way, and holding out its arms stiffly, as if in salutation.

Recovering from their fear, the girls advanced again, Peggy giggling nervously. "I thought it was him!" she whispered.

"He, not him," was on Margaret's lips, but she kept the words back.

She could not always be a schoolmistress; and then she scorned herself for moral cowardice.

"Thought it was who, Peggy?" she asked. "Hugo Montfort?"

"Ye—yes!" said Peggy.

"But he did not hang himself, child! He wants to find his papers, that is all. Ah, here are the trunks; now for the wigs, girls!"

The wig trunk proved a most delightful repository. The wigs were in neat boxes; many of them were of horsehair, but a few were of human hair, frizzed and tortured out of all softness or beauty. Dainty Margaret did not incline to put them on, but Peggy was soon glorious in a huge white structure, with a wreath of roses on the top, that made her look twice her height. "Ain't I fine?" she cried. "Here, Margaret, here is one for you."

Margaret twirled the wig around, and examined it curiously. "What they all must have looked like!" she said. "This is a judge's wig, I think."

"Then it can fit none but you, Señorita Perfecta!" cried Rita; but the sting was gone from her tone, and she had wholly forgotten her moment of spite. "Here! here is mine. Behold me, a gallant of the court! I advance, I bow—but my cloak, where is my cloak? Quick, Marguerite, the key of the other chest!"

The other chest, a great black one, studded with brass nails, contained, as Mrs. Cheriton had said, any amount of material for the delightful pastime of dressing up. The gauzes were crumpled, to be sure, the gold lace tarnished, and the satins and brocades more or less spotted and decayed; but what of that? The splendours of the Family Chest were too solemn to sport with; here was material for hours and days of joy. Rita was soon arrayed in a scarlet military coat, a habit skirt of dark velvet, and a plumed hat which perched like a bird on top of her flowing wig. Peggy was put into a charming Watteau costume of flowered silk, in which she looked so pretty that Rita declared it was a shame for her ever to wear anything else; while Margaret found a long, gold-spotted gauze that took her fancy mightily. Thus attired, the three girls frisked and danced about the huge, dim old garret, astonishing the spiders, and sending the mice scuttling into their holes in terror. The seventeen years that sometimes weighed heavily on Margaret's slender shoulders, and that sat like a flame of pride on Rita's white forehead, seemed utterly forgotten; these were three merry children that ran to and fro, waking the echoes to mirth. Rita proposed a dance, and cried out in horror when Peggy confessed that she could not dance at all, and Margaret that she had had few lessons and no experience.

"Poor victims!" cried the Cuban. "Slaves of Northern prejudice! I will teach you, my poors! Not to dance, not to understand the management of a fan—how are you to go through life, without equipment, I ask you?"

She held out her arms with a gesture so tragic that Margaret could not help laughing.

"Rita, forgive me!" she said. "I was trying to fancy my poor dear father giving me a lesson in the management of a fan. He was really my chief teacher, you know."

"Yes, and who was there for me to dance with?" cried Peggy, holding out her gay flounces. "Brother Jim would be rather like a grizzly bear, I think, and none of the others would. Jean and I used to dance with each other, but it was just jumping up and down, for we didn't know anything else."

Rita sighed, and felt the weight of empire on her shoulders. "You shall learn," she said again. "I will teach you. But not here, it is too dim and dusty. The courtesy, however, we can try. Mesdames! Raise the skirt, thus, the left foot in advance; the left, Peggy, child of despair! now bend the right knee, and slowly, slowly, sink thus, with grace and dignity. Oh, pity on me, what have you done now?"

Poor Peggy had done her best, but when it came to sinking slowly and gracefully, it was too much for her. She stepped on her train, tripped, lost her balance, and fell heavily back against the wall. She clutched the wooden panel behind her, and felt it move under her fingers.

"Oh, mercy!" she cried, "it's moving! The wall is moving! Margaret, catch hold of my hand!"

Margaret caught her hand, and helped her to her feet. When she moved away from the wall, it was seen that the wooden panel had indeed moved. It had slid open a few inches, and blackness looked through at them. Peggy clutched her cousins and trembled. Where was now the courage, the coolness, which had made her the heroine of the morning's adventure? Gone! Anything in the ordinary course of nature, bogs and such matters, Peggy was mistress of, but black spaces, with possible white figures lurking in them, were out of her province.

"Margaret," she whispered, "do you see? It is open!"

"Yes, I see!" said Margaret. "What a delightfully mysterious thing, girls! A secret chamber, perhaps, or a staircase! It must be a staircase, for it is in the thickness of the wall behind the chimney. Do run and get a lamp, Peggy, like a good girl, and we will see. How damp and earthy it smells!"

Peggy flew, only too glad to get away from the black, yawning hole. She was back in three minutes with the lamp, and the three cousins peered into the open space, Margaret holding the lamp high above her head, so that the light might penetrate as far as possible.

It was indeed a staircase; a narrow, winding way, wide enough for one person, but no more. It plunged down like a black pit, and its end could not be seen.

"But this is superb!" cried Margaret. "Shall we explore it, girls? I don't suppose there can be any objection, do you? It is probably never used."

"By all means, let us explore!" said Rita. "But do you know what I am thinking, Marguerite?"

"Something romantic and mysterious, I am sure!" said Margaret, smiling.

"Something practical and businesslike, rather, très chère. I am thinking that for a concealment, if a concealment were necessary, this is the finest house in the world. Come on!"

Peggy hung back, her round cheeks pale with dread; but she could not bear to be left behind; and as Margaret and Rita plunged down the narrow stair, she followed, with beating heart. She had longed all her breezy little life for mystery, adventure, something wonderful to happen to her, with which she could impress and awe the younger children; now it had really come, and her heart beat with mingled terror and excitement.

Down—down—down. The lamplight shone on the rough walls of discoloured plaster, the old steps creaked beneath their tread; that was all. Now they came to a tiny landing, and something gleamed before them,—the brass handle of a door. Margaret hesitated, fearing that they might be trenching on forbidden ground; but Rita opened the door quickly, and Peggy pressed down behind her.

They saw a room, like the other bedrooms in the house, large and airy. It was evidently ready for use, the bed neatly made, everything in spotless order. Brushes and shaving-tools lay on the dressing-bureau. The table was covered with books.

"Uncle John's room!" whispered Margaret. "It must be, of course; and this is where the locked door is on the second story. Come along, girls; we ought not to go prying into people's rooms!"

"My faith, I cannot see that!" retorted Rita. "If there were anything of interest in the room,—but nothing—a plain room, and nothing more! A pretty thing to end a secret staircase; he should have shame for it. But come, as you say; we have yet a way to go down."

They closed the door carefully, and once more began the descent. Down—down—down. But this second half of the way was different. The staircase was wider, and the walls were cased in wood. Moreover, it showed marks of usage. The steps above were covered with thick dust, evidently long undisturbed; but these were clean and shining. Decidedly, the mystery was deepening.

"Suppose we find it is just a back way to the servants' rooms!" whispered practical Margaret.

"Suppose feedle-dee-dee!" said Rita; and her funny little foreign accent on the word made Peggy choke and splutter behind her.

Now they were evidently approaching the ground floor, for sounds were audible below them: a footstep, and then the clink of metal, as if some one were moving fire-irons.

"Elizabeth, probably!" whispered Margaret. "What shall we say to her?"

"Let's yell and rush out and scare her!" proposed Peggy.

"Hush!" said Rita. "Oh, hush! we know not who it is. Look! a gleam of light,—the crack of a door! quick, the lamp!" and with a swift, silent breath she blew out the lamp, and they were in total darkness.

They now saw plainly the light that shone through the crack of a door, a few steps below them. The sounds in the room beneath had ceased. All was still for a moment; then suddenly Peggy made a false step in the dark, and stumbled; she uttered a smothered shriek, and then began to giggle.

"Animal!" muttered Rita through her teeth. "Can you not be silent?"

Peggy was now in front, and seeing that light came also through the keyhole, she stooped and looked through it. The next instant she uttered a dreadful shriek, and staggered back into Margaret's arms. "The man!" she cried; "the man in black velvet!"

A chair was hastily pushed back in the room below; steps crossed the floor, and as Margaret flung open the door, another door at the further end of the room was seen to close softly.

CHAPTER VIII

CUBA LIBRE

"But, Marguerite, when I tell you that I know!"

"But, Rita, my dear, how can you know?"

"Look at me; listen to me! Have you your senses?"

"Most of them, I hope."

"Very well, then, attend! When stupid, stupid Peggy—I love her, observe; she is my sister, but we must admit that she is stupid,—truth, Marguerite, is the jewel of my soul—when she stumbled against the door, when she screamed, we heard sounds, did we not?"

"We did!" Margaret admitted.

"Sounds,—and what sounds? Not the broom of a servant, not the rustle of a dress,—no, we hear the step of a man! We enter, and a door closes at the further end of the room; click, a lock snaps! I rush to the window; a figure disappears around the corner of the house; I cannot see what it is, but I would swear it was no woman. I return,—we look about us at this room, which never have we seen before. A gentleman's room, as an infant could perceive. A private library, study, what you will, luxurious, enchanting. Books over which you sob with emotion,—or would sob, if your temperament permitted you expression; pictures that fill my soul with enchantment; a writing-table, and on it papers—heaps and mounds of papers! Am I right? do I exaggerate? Alps, Pyrenees of papers! You saw them?"

"I didn't see anything higher than Mt. Washington," said Margaret soberly. "There were a good many, I confess."

"They burst from drawers," pursued Rita, enjoying herself immensely; "they toppled like snow-drifts; they strewed the floor to a depth of—"

"Oh, Rita, Rita! do rein your Pegasus in, or he will fly away altogether. There certainly were a great many papers, and they confirmed our poor little Peggy in her belief that the man she had seen was Hugo Montfort, making his ghostly search for the papers he lost. Whereas you think—"

"Think! when I tell you that I know!"

"You think," Margaret went on calmly, "that it was John Strong, the gardener. Well, and what if it was?"

"What if it was? Marguerite, you are impossible; you have the intelligence of a babe new born. What! we find this man in his master's room, spying upon his private things, romaging—what is that word?—romaging his papers, most likely making himself possessed of what he will, and you say, what of this? Caramba, I will tell you what of this it would be in Cuba! String him up to the wall and give him quick fifty lashes; that would be of it!"

"Long Island is a good way from Cuba!" said Margaret. "I don't think we will try anything of that sort here, Rita. And when you come to think of it, my dear, we have been here a few weeks, and John Strong was here before we were born; Aunt Faith told me so. Don't you think he may perhaps know what he is about rather better than we do?"

"Know what he is about!" Rita protested, with a shower of nods, that he knew very well what he was about. The question was, did their uncle know? And the black velvet coat, what had Margaret to say to that? she demanded. It was evident that this good man, this worthy servant, was in the habit of wearing his master's clothes during his absence. Did gardeners habitually appear in black velvet? Ha! tell her that!

Margaret did not know that they did, but it was perfectly possible that Mr. Montfort might have given some of his old clothes, a cast-off smoking-jacket, for example, to his gardener and confidential servant. There would be nothing remarkable in that, surely. Besides, were they absolutely certain that the mysterious individual was dressed in black velvet? Poor, dear Peggy was in such a state of excitement, she might well have fancied—and so on, and so on. The two cousins went over the ground again and again, but could come to no decision.

"Say what you will, très chère!" said Rita, finally; "glorify your gardener, give him the family wardrobe, the family papers; I keep watch on him, that is all! Let Master Strong beware! Not for nothing was I brought up on a plantation. Have I not known overseers, to say nothing of hosts of servants, white, black, yellow? Your books, chère Marguerite, do they teach you the knowledge of persons? Let him beware! he knows not a Cuban!" and she nodded, and bent her brows so tragically that Margaret could hardly keep her countenance.

"Have you ever acted, Rita?" she asked, following the train of her thoughts. "I am sure you must do it so well."

"Mi alma!" cried Rita, "it was my joy! Conchita and I—ahi! what plays we have acted in the myrtle-bower in the garden! Will you see me act? You shall."

John Strong and his iniquities were forgotten in a moment. Bidding Margaret call Peggy, and make themselves into an audience in the lower hall, Rita whirled away to her own room, where they could hear her singing to herself, and pulling open drawers with reckless ardour. The two other girls ensconced themselves in a window-seat of the hall and waited.

"Do you know what she is going to do?" asked Peggy.

Margaret shook her head. "Something pretty and graceful, no doubt. She is a born actress, you know."

"I never saw an actress," said Peggy. "She—she is awfully fascinating, Margaret, isn't she?"

Margaret assented warmly. There was no tinge of jealousy in her composition, or she might have felt a slight pang at the tone of admiring awe in which Peggy now spoke of her Cuban cousin. Things were changed indeed since the night of their arrival.

"It isn't only that she is so awfully pretty," Peggy went on, "but she moves so—and her voice is so soft, and—oh, Margaret, do you suppose I can ever be the least like her, just the least bit in the world?"

She looked anxiously at Margaret, who gazed back affectionately at her, at the round, rosy childish face, the little tilted nose, the fluffy, fair hair. It seemed the most natural thing in the world to stroke and pat Peggy as if she were a kitten, but no one would think of patting Rita.

"Dear," said Margaret softly, "dear Peggy! I like you better as you are. Of course Rita is very beautiful, and neither you nor I could ever look in the least like her, Peggy. But—it is a great deal better to look like our own selves, isn't it, and learn to appear at our best in a way that suits us? That is what I think. Now that you have learned to do your hair so nicely, and to keep your dress neat—"

"You taught me that," said honest Peggy; "you taught me all that, Margaret. I was a perfect pig when I came here; you know I was."

"Don't call my cousin names, miss! I cannot permit it. But if I have taught you anything, Peggy, it is Rita who has given you the little graces that you have been picking up. I never could have taught you to bow,—and really, you are quite superb since the last lesson. Then, these pretty dresses—"

"Oh, do you think I ought to take them?" broke in Peggy. "Margaret, do you think so? She brought them into my room, you know, and flung them down in a heap, and said they were only fit for dust-cloths—you know the way she talks, dear thing. The lovely brown crepon, she said it was the most hideous thing she had ever seen, and that it was the deed of an assassin to offer it to me. And when I said I couldn't take so many, she snatched up the scissors, and was going to cut them all up—she really was, Margaret. What could I do?"

"Nothing, dear child, except take them, I really think. It was a real pleasure to Rita to give them to you, I am sure, and she could not possibly wear a quarter of all the gowns she brought here. But see, here comes our bird of paradise herself. Now we shall see something lovely!"

Rita came down the stairs, singing a little Spanish song. Her dress of black gauze fluttered in wide breezy folds, a gauze scarf floated from her shoulders; she was indeed a vision of beauty, and the two cousins gazed at her with delight. Advancing into the middle of the hall, she swept a splendid courtesy, and suddenly unfurled a huge scarlet fan. With this, she proceeded to go through a series of astonishing performances. She danced with it, she sang with it. She closed it, and it was a dagger, and she swooped upon an invisible enemy, and stabbed him to the heart; she flung it open, and it became the messenger of love, over which her black eyes gleamed and glowed in irresistible coquetry. All the time she kept up a dramatic chant, sometimes sinking almost to a whisper, again rising to a shriek of joy or passion. Suddenly she stopped.

"All this is play!" she said, turning to her rapt audience.

"Now you shall see the real thing: you shall see Cuba libre. But for this I must have another person; it is impossible to do it alone. Margaret,—no! Peggy can better do this! Peggy, come, and you shall be Spain, the tyrant."

Peggy looked as if she would much rather be aspiring Cuba, but she came forward obediently, and was bidden to put herself in an attitude of insolent defiance. Peggy scowled and doubled up her fists, thinking of a picture of a prizefighter that she had once seen.

"Ah!" cried Rita, springing upon her. "Not thus! you have the air of a cross child. Thus, do you see? Fold the arms upon the chest, abase the head, bring the eyebrows down till you have to look through them! So! that is better! Now gnaw your under lip, and draw in your breath with a hiss, thus!" and Rita herself uttered a hiss so malignant that poor Peggy started back in affright. "But be still!" cried Rita, "you are now perfect. You are an object—is she not, Marguerite?—to turn cold the blood." Margaret did not commit herself, being wholly occupied in keeping back the smiles that Peggy's aspect called forth. She certainly was an object, poor dear child, but Rita was so absorbed in her play that she saw nothing absurd even in a tyrant scowling through flaxen eyebrows with a pair of helpless, frightened blue eyes. She now drew back, knelt, flung up her arms, and raised her eyes to heaven. Her lips moved; she was praying for the success of her cause. Rising, she came forward, and with noble earnestness demanded her freedom. The tyrant was bidden to look about on the ruin and desolation that he had wrought; he was implored by all that was holy, all that was just and noble, to withdraw from the land where he had long ceased to have any real right of ownership. Peggy, in obedience to whispered orders, shook her head with stubborn violence, and stamped her foot. Cuba then, drawing herself to her full height, threw down her gage of defiance (a tiny pearl-covered glove) and declared war to extermination. The banner of freedom (the fan) was unfurled and waved on high, the national song was chanted, and the war began. Spain, the tyrant, now had a hard time of it. She was pounced upon from one side, then from another; she was surrounded, hustled this way and that; the fan was fluttered wide in her face, poked sharply between her ribs. A single straightforward blow from her strong young arm would have laid the slender Cuba at her feet, but she could strike no blow. She was only to hiss, and clutch the air in impotent fury, and when she did this, Margaret had such an uncontrollable fit of coughing that it almost produced an armistice.

Now Spain was told that she was growing weak, a decrepit, bleeding old woman. Her fate was upon her; let her die!

Obeying the imperious gesture, Peggy sank on her knees, and had the satisfaction of hearing that "the old serpent died bravely." The fan did more and more dreadful execution, and now she lay gasping, dying, on the floor. Standing above her was a triumphant young goddess, waving the flag of Cuba libre, and declaring, with her foot on the neck of the prostrate tyrant, that despotism was dead, and that Freedom was descending from heaven, robed in the Cuban colours, and surrounded by a choir of angels, all singing the national anthem. And here Rita actually pulled from her bosom a small flag showing the Cuban colours, and waved it, crying that the blood-red banner of war (the fan) was now furled forever, and that Cuba and the United States, now twin sisters, would proceed to rule the world after the most approved methods. This ended the scene, and the two actors stood before Margaret, one very red and sheepish, the other glowing like flame with pride and enthusiasm, awaiting her plaudits. Margaret clapped and shouted as loud as she could, and expressed her admiration warmly enough; but Rita shook her head and sighed.

"Ah, for an audience!" she cried. "To pour out one's heart, to live the life of one's country, and have but one to see it,—it is sad, it is tragic. Do I exaggerate, Marguerite?—it is death-dealing!" Then she praised Peggy, and told her that she had made a magnificent tyrant, and had died as game as possible. "Ah!" she said. "What it would be if you could only do something real for Cuba! I would shed my blood, would pour out its ultimate drops (Rita's idioms were apt to become foreign when she was excited), but if you also could do something, my cousins, what glory, what joy for you; and it may be possible. No, hush! not a word! At present, I breathe not a whisper, I am the grave. But there may come a day, an hour, when I shall call to you with the voice of a trumpet; and you,—you will awaken, halves of my heart; you will spring to my side, you will— Marguerite, you are laughing! At what, I ask you?"

"I beg your pardon, dear," said Margaret. "I was only thinking that a trumpet might really be needed, since a bell is not loud enough. The dinner-bell rang five minutes ago, and Elizabeth has come to see what we are about."

But at sight of Elizabeth, standing demurely in the doorway, Cuba libre vanished, and there remained only a very pretty young lady in the sulks, who had to be coaxed for five minutes more before she would come to her dinner.

"Am I seventeen, or thirty-seven?" thought Margaret, as she finally led the way to the dining-room.

CHAPTER IX

DAY BY DAY

> "Oh! what a mystery
> The study is of history!"

For some time things continued to go smoothly and pleasantly at Fernley. The days slipped away, with nothing special to mark any one, but all bright with flowers and gay with laughter. The three girls were excellent friends, and grew to understand each other better and better. The morning belonged rather to Margaret and Peggy; Rita was always late, and often preferred to have her breakfast brought to her room, a practice of which the other girls disapproved highly. They were always out in the garden by half past eight, with breakfast a thing of the past, and the day before them. The stocking-basket generally came with them, and waited patiently in a corner of the green summer-house while they took their "constitutional," which often consisted of a run through the waving fields, or a walk along the top of the broad stone wall that ran around the garden; or again, a tree-top excursion, as they called it, in the great swing under the chestnut-trees. Then, while they mended their stockings, Margaret would give Peggy a "talk-lesson," the only kind that she was willing to receive, on English history, with an occasional digression to the Trojan war, or the Norse mythology, as the case might be. Peggy detested history, and knew next to nothing of it, and this was a grievous thing to Margaret.

> "First William the Norman,
> Then William his son;
> Henry, Stephen and Henry,
> Then Richard and John,"

had been one of her own nursery rhymes, and she could not understand any one's not thrilling responsive when the great names were spoken that filled her with awe and joy, or with burning resentment.

"But, my dear," she would cry, when Peggy yawned at Canute, and said he was an old stupid, "my dear, think of the place he holds! think of the things he did!"

"Well, he's dead!" Peggy would reply; "I don't see what good it does to bother about him now. Who cares what he did, all that time ago?"

"But," Margaret explained patiently, "if he had not done the things, Peggy, don't you see, everything would have been different. We must know, mustn't we, how it all came about that our life is what it is now? We must see what we came from, and who the men were that made the changes, and brought us on and up."

"I don't see why!" said Peggy; "I don't see what difference it makes to me that Alfred played the harp. I don't want to play the harp, and I never saw any one who did. It is rather fun about the cakes, but he was awfully stupid to let them burn, seems to me."

Not a thrill could Margaret awaken by any recital of the sorrows and sufferings of the Boy Kings, or even of her favourite Prince Arthur. When her voice broke in the recital of his piteous tale, Peggy would look up at her coolly and say, "How horrid of them! But he would have been dead by this time anyway, Margaret; why do you care so much?"

Still Margaret persevered, never losing hope, simply because she could not believe that the subject itself could fail to interest any one in his senses. It was her own fault a good deal, she tried to think; she did not tell the story right, or her voice was too monotonous,— Papa was always telling her to put more colour into her reading,— or something. The history itself could not be at fault.

"And, Peggy dear; don't think I want to be lecturing you all the time, but—these are things that one has to know something about, or one will appear uneducated, and you don't want to do that."

"I don't care. I don't see the use of this kind of education, Margaret, and that is just the truth. Ma never had any of what you call education,—she was a farmer's daughter, you know, and had always lived on the prairie,—and she has always got on well enough. Hugh talks just like you do—"

"Please, dear, as you do, not like."

"Well, as you do, then. He talks William the Conqueror and all those old fuddy-duddies by the yard, but he can't make me see the use of them, and you can't. Now if you would give me some mathematics; that is what I want. If you would give me some solid geometry, Margaret!"

But here poor Margaret hung her head and blushed, and confessed that she had no solid geometry to give. Her geometry had been fluid, or rather, vapourous, and had floated away, unthought of and unregretted.

"I am sorry and ashamed," she said. "Of course I ought to be able to teach it, and if I go into a school, of course I shall have to study again and make it up, so that I can. But it never can be possible that triangles should be as interesting as human beings, Peggy."

"A great deal more interesting," Peggy maintained, "when the human beings are dead and buried hundreds of years."

"One word more, and I have done," said poor Margaret. "You used an expression, dear,—old fuddy-duddies, was it? I never heard it before. Do you think it is an elegant expression, Peggy dear?"

"It's as good as I am girl!" said Peggy; and Margaret shut her eyes, and felt despair in her heart. But soon she felt a warm kiss on her forehead, and Peggy was promising to be good, and to try harder, and even to do her best to learn the difference between the two Harolds,—Hardrada and Godwinsson.

And if she would promise to do that, might she just climb up now and see what that nest was, out on the fork there?

Perhaps Rita would come down soon, with her guitar or her embroidery-frame; and they would sing and chatter till the early dinner. Rita's songs were all of love and war, boleros and bull-fights. She sang them with flashing ardour, and the other girls heard with breathless delight, watching the play of colour and feeling, that made her face a living transcript of what she sang. But when she was tired, she would hand the guitar to Margaret, and beg her to sing "something cool, peaceful, sea-green, like yourself, Marguerite!"

"Am I sea-green?" asked Margaret.

"Ah! cherub! you understand me! My blood is in a fever with these songs of Cuba. I want coolness, icy caves, pine-trees in the wind!"

So Margaret would take the guitar, and sing in her calm, smooth contralto the songs her father used to love: songs of the North, that had indeed the sound of the sea and the wind in them.

> "It was all for our rightful king
> That we left fair Scotland's strand.
> It was all for our rightful king,
> We ever saw Irish land,
> My dear,
> We ever saw Irish land!"

The plaintive melody rose and fell like the waves on the shore; and Rita would curl herself like a panther in the sun, and murmur with pleasure, and call for more. Then, perhaps, Margaret would sing that lovely ballad of Hogg's, which begins,

> "Far down by yon hills of the heather sae green,
> And down by the corrie that sings to the sea,
> The bonnie young Flora sat sighing her lane,
> The dew on her plaid and the tear in her e'e.
> "She looked on a boat with the breezes that swung
> Afar on the wave, like a bird on the main,

And aye as it lessened, she sighed and she sung,
'Fareweel to the lad I shall ne'er see again!'"

But Rita had no patience with Flora McDonald.

"Why did she not go with him?" she asked, when Margaret, after the song was over, told the brave story of Prince Charlie's escape after Culloden, and of how the noble girl, at the risk of her own life, led the prince, disguised as her waiting-woman, through many weary ways, till they reached the seashore where the vessel was waiting to take him to France.

"He could not speak!" said Margaret. "He just took her hand, and stood looking at her; but she could hardly see him for her tears. Then he took off his cap, and stooped down and kissed her twice on the forehead; and so he went. But after he was in the boat, he turned again, and said to her:

"'After all that has happened, I still hope, madam, we shall meet in St. James's yet!' But of course they never did."

"But why did she not go with him?" demanded Rita. "She had spirit, it appears. Why did she let him go without her?"

Margaret gazed at her wide-eyed.

"He was going into exile," she said. "She had done all she could, she had saved his life; there was nothing more to be done."

"But—that she should leave him! Did she not love him? was he faithless?"

Margaret blushed, and drew herself up unconsciously. "You do not understand, Rita," she said gravely. "This was her prince, the son of her sovereign; she was a simple Scottish gentlewoman. When he was flying for his life, she was able to befriend him, and to save his life at peril of her own; but when that was over, there was no more need of her, and she went back to her home. What should she have done in France, at the king's court?"

"Even if so," muttered Rita, with the well-known shrug of her shoulders, "I would have gone, if it had been I. He should not have thrown me off like that."

Margaret raised her eyes, full of angry light, and opened her lips to speak; but instead kept silence for a moment. Then, "You do not understand," she said again, but gently; "my mother was a Scotchwoman, so I feel differently, of course. It is no matter, but I will tell you this about Miss McDonald: that when she died, years after, an old woman of seventy, she was buried in the sheet that had covered Prince Charles Stuart, that night after Culloden."

"My!" said Peggy, "it must have been awfully yellow!"

After dinner it was Rita's custom to take a siesta. She declared that she required more sleep than most people, and that without eleven hours' repose she should perish. So while she slept, Margaret and Peggy arranged flowers, or Peggy would write home, with many sighs of weariness and distress, while Margaret, sitting near her, snatched a half-hour for some enchanting book. It sometimes seemed to her more than she could bear, to be among so many fine books, and to have almost no time to read. At home, several hours were spent in reading, as a matter of course; often and often, the long, happy evening would pass without a word exchanged between her father and herself. Only, when either looked up from the book, there was always the meeting glance of love and sympathy, which made the printed page shine golden when the eyes returned to it. Here, reading was considered a singular waste of time. Rita read herself to sleep with a novel, but Peggy was entirely frank in her confession that she should not care if she never saw a book again. Even the home letters were a grievous task to her, for she never could think of anything to say. Margaret, deep in the precious pages of Froissart, it might be, would be roused by a portentous sigh, and looking up, would find Peggy champing the penhandle, and gazing at her with lack-lustre eyes.

"What's the matter now, Peg of Limavaddy?"

"I can't—think—of a single thing to say."

"Child! I thought you had so much to tell them this time. Think of that lovely drive we took yesterday; I thought you were going to tell about that. Don't you remember the sunset from the top of the long hill, and how we made believe the clouds were our fairy castles, and each said what she would do when she got there? Rita was going to organise a Sunset Dance, with ten thousand fairies in crimson and gold, and you were going to be met by a hundred thoroughbred horses, all white as snow, and were going to drive them abreast in a golden chariot; don't you remember all that? Tell them about the drive!"

"I have told them," said Peggy gloomily. "I couldn't put in all that, Margaret; it would take all day, and besides, Ma would think I was crazy."

"Do you mind my seeing what you wrote?—oh, Peggy!"

For Peggy had written this: "We had an elagant ride yesterday."

"What's the matter?" asked Peggy. "Isn't it spelled right?"

"Oh, that isn't it!" said Margaret. "At least, that is the smallest part. 'Elegant' has two e's, not two a's. But,—Peggy dear, you surely would not speak of a drive as elegant!"

"Why not? I said ride, not drive, but I don't see any difference. It was elegant; you said so yourself. I don't understand what you mean, Margaret." And Peggy looked injured, and began to hunch her shoulders and put out her under lip; but for once Margaret, wounded in a tender part, took no heed of the signs of coming trouble.

"I say so? Never!" she cried indignantly. "I hope I—that is, I—I don't think the word can be used in that way, Peggy; I do not, indeed. You speak of an elegant dress, or an elegant woman, but not of an elegant drive or an elegant sunset. The word implies something refined, something—"

"Oh, bother!" said Peggy rudely. "I didn't come here to school, Margaret Montfort!"

"I sometimes wonder if you ever went anywhere to school!" said Margaret; and she took her book and went away without another word, her heart beating high with anger and impatience.

Such affairs were short-lived, however. Margaret had too much sense and good feeling, Peggy too much affection, to let them last. The kiss and the kind word were not long in following, and it was to be noticed that Rita was never allowed to find out that her two Northern cousins ever disagreed by so much as a word. There was some unspoken bond that bade them both make common cause before the foreign cousin whom both loved and admired. So when Rita made her appearance beautifully dressed for the afternoon drive or walk (for they could not have the good white horse every day,—a fact which made the señorita chafe and rage against John Strong more than ever), she always found smiling faces to welcome her, and the three would go off together in high spirits, to explore some new and lovely part of the country.

Peggy was always the driver. On their first drive John Strong had gone with them, to the intense disgust of Rita, and the indignation of Peggy, who, though she was very fond of the grave factotum, resented the doubt he implied of her skill. It was a silent drive, Margaret alone responding to the remarks of their conductor, as he pointed out this or that beautiful view. He never went with them again, but having first tested Peggy's powers by a tête-à-tête drive with her, cheerfully resigned the reins, and used to watch their departure with calm approval.

"The little one makes much the best figure on the box!" John Strong would say to himself. "If life were all driving, now—but—

> "Weel I ken my ain lassie;
> Kind love is in her e'e!"

CHAPTER X

LOOKING BACKWARD

But in the twilight came Margaret's hour of comfort. Then Peggy had her dancing-lesson from Rita, and while the two were whirling and stumping about the hall, she would steal away through the little door and down the three steps to the white rooms, where peace and quiet, gentle words and kind affection were always awaiting her. Aunt Faith always understood the little troubles, and had the right word to say, of sympathy or counsel. The two had grown very near to each other.

"How is it," Margaret asked one evening, "I seem so much nearer your age, Aunt Faith, than the girls'? Do you suppose I really belong to your generation, and got left behind by accident?"

Aunt Faith laughed. "My dear, you ought to have had half a dozen brothers and sisters!" she said. "An only child grows up too fast, especially where, as in your case, the companionship with father or mother is close and intimate. No doubt your dear father did his best to grow down to your age, when you were little; but he did not succeed, I fear, so you had to grow up to his. Was not that the way?"

Margaret nodded thoughtfully. "I remember his playing horse with me!" she said. "Poor dear Papa! I asked him to play, and he said in his deep, slow way, 'Surely! surely! the child must have play. Play is necessary for development.' And then he sat and looked at me, with his Greek book in his hand, as if I were a word that he could not find the meaning of. Oh! I remember it so well, though I must have been a little tot. Then he got up and said, 'I will be a horse, Margaret! Consider me a horse!' and he gave me the tassels of his dressing-gown, and began to amble about the room slowly, among the piles of books. Oh, dear! I can see him now, dear Papa! He made a very slow horse, Aunt Faith, and I felt, in a baby way, that there was something awful about it, and that he was not meant to play. I think I must have dropped the tassels pretty soon, for he came to a great book lying open on a chair, and forgot everything else, and stood there for an hour reading it. I never asked him to play again, but we used to laugh over it when we were big—I mean when I was big, and had grown up to him a little bit."

Mrs. Cheriton laid her hand on the girl's head, and smoothed her hair tenderly.

"You must have been lonely sometimes, dear?" she said.

"Oh, no; never, I think. You see, I learned so many things that I could play by myself, and it never troubled Papa to have me in the room where he was writing; I think he rather liked it. I had the waste-paper basket; that was one of my chief delights. I might do what I wanted with the papers, if I only put them back. So I carpeted the room with them, and I laid out streets and squares, and had the pamphlets for walls and houses. Or I was a queen, with a great correspondence, and all the letters were brought to me by pages in green and gold, and when I read them (this was before I could really read, of course), they were all from my baby sister, and they told of all the lovely things she was seeing, and the wonderful countries she and Mamma were travelling in. Aunt Faith, I never see a waste-paper basket now, without feeling as if there must be a letter for me in it."

"Was there really a baby sister, dear?"

"Yes, oh, yes! she died with Mamma, only a few days after her birth,—little Penelope! It seems such a great name for a tiny baby, doesn't it, Aunt Faith? But it is a family name, Papa told me."

"Yes, indeed, many of the Montforts have been named Penelope. You remember the poor Aunt Penelope I told you about, who made the unhappy marriage; and there were many others."

"Oh, that reminds me!" said Margaret. "Aunt Faith, you promised to tell me some day about Aunt Phoebe. Don't you remember? We were speaking of these white rooms, and you said it was a fancy of Uncle John's to have them so, and you thought he remembered his Great-aunt Phoebe; and then you said you would tell me some time, and this is some time, isn't it, Auntie dear?"

"I cannot deny that, Margaret, certainly. And I don't know why this is not a very good time; the twilight is soft and dusky, and Aunt Phoebe's story ought not to be told in broad daylight."

She was silent a moment, as if looking back into the past. "It is the sequel, rather than the story itself, that is singular," she said. "The first part is like only too many other stories, alas! Your Great-aunt Phoebe—your Great-great-aunt, I should say—was betrothed to a brave young officer, Lieutenant Hetherington. It was just at the breaking out of the War of 1812, and the engagement was made just as he was going into active service. She was a beautiful girl, with large dark eyes, and superb fair hair,—none of you three girls have this combination, but it is not uncommon among the Montforts; I myself had fair hair and dark eyes. Phoebe was highly romantic, and when her lover went to war, she gave him a sword-belt plaited of her own hair."

"Oh," cried Margaret, "like Sir Percival's sister!"

"Exactly! Very likely it was from that story that she took the idea, for she was a great reader. However it might be, her mother was greatly distressed at her cutting off so much of her fine hair, and did her best to prevent it, but to no purpose, as you may imagine. Giles Hetherington joined the army, carrying the braided belt with him, and they say he never parted with it, night or day, but slept with it beside him on the pillow. Poor fellow! He was killed in a night attack by the Indians, set on by the British. He was in a hut with some other officers, and the sentry must have slept at his post, they supposed. They were surrounded, the house set on fire, and the officers all killed. One private escaped to tell the dreadful story, and he told of the gallant fight they made, and how Giles Hetherington fought for the life that was so dear to others. He defended the door while two of his comrades forced the window open, hoping to steal around and take the savages in the rear; but the window was watched, too, and these officers were shot down, and then an Indian sprang in at the window, and stabbed Hetherington in the back. Ah, me! It is a terrible story, dear child! He staggered back to the bed, the soldier said, and caught up the belt, that was lying there while he slept. He was past speech, but he gave it to this soldier, who was a lad from this place, and motioned him to the window; then he fell back dead, and the man crept out of the window,—the Indians having run around to the front,—and crawled off, lying flat in the grass, and so escaped with his life. He brought the belt, all dabbled with blood, back to Fernley, meaning to give it to Madam Montfort quietly, that she might break the news to her daughter, but poor Phoebe chanced to come through the garden just as he was standing on the steps with the belt in his hand, and she saw it."

"Oh! oh, dear!" cried Margaret, clasping her hands. "Aunt Faith, it is too dreadful! How could she bear it?"

"My dear, she could not bear it. She had not the strength. She did not lose her mind, like poor Aunt Penelope, but really, it might almost have been as well if she had, poor soul. When she woke from the long swoon into which she had fallen at sight of the belt, she heard all the story through without a word, and then she came here, and left the world."

"Came here?" repeated Margaret.

"Here, to these rooms; but what different rooms! She sent for a painter, and had the walls painted black. She had everything with an atom of colour in it taken away; and in these black rooms she lived, and in them she died. She wept so much—partly that, and partly the want of light—that her eyes became abnormally sensitive, and she could not bear even to see anything white. As time went on—Margaret, you will hardly believe this, but it is literally true—she would not even have white china on her table. She declared it hurt her eyes. So her father, who could refuse her nothing, sent for a set of dark brown china, and she ate brown bread on it,—would not look at white bread,—and was served by a mulatto woman, an old nurse who had been in the family from her childhood."

"Aunt Faith, can it be—you say it really is true! but—how could they let her? Why did they not have an oculist?"

"My dear child, oculists did not exist in those days. If she were living to-day, it would be pronounced a case of nervous exhaustion, and she would be taken for a sea voyage, or sent to a rest-cure, or treated in one of the hundred different ways that we know of nowadays. But then, nobody knew what to do for her, poor lady. To be 'crossed in love,' as it was called, was a thing that admitted of no cure, unless the patient were willing to be cured. People spoke of Phoebe Montfort under their breath, and called her 'a blight,' meaning a person whose life has been blighted. The world has gone on a good deal in the two generations since then, my dear Margaret."

"I should think so," said Margaret; "poor soul! And did she have to live very long, Aunt Faith? I hope not!"

"A good many years, my dear. She must have been an elderly woman when she died; not old, as I count age, but perhaps seventy-five, or thereabouts. I lived far away at that time, but John Montfort has often told me of the time of her death. He was a little lad, and he regarded the Black Rooms and their tenant with the utmost terror. He used to run past the door, he says, for fear the Black Aunt should come out and seize him, and take him into her dreary dwelling. Poor Aunt Phoebe was the mildest creature in the world, and would not have hurt a fly, but to him she was something awful,—out of nature. He was taken in to see her once or twice a year, and he always had nightmare after it, being a nervous child. Well, one day he was running through the Green Parlour here, and looking back at the windows of the Black Rooms, as he never could help doing; and he saw Rosalie, the coloured woman, come to the window and throw it wide open, letting in the full light of day.

Then she went to the next, and so on; and the child knew what had happened before she spoke. I remember her words:

"'She's gone, honey! Her sperit's gone. It went out'n dis window, straight by whar you's standin', and into the cedar bush. De Lord hab mercy!'

"And poor little John took to his heels, and ran, and never stopped running till he was in his own bed upstairs.

"That is the story, Margaret; but I ought to add that the belt of hair was laid in the grave with her, at her special request."

"What a sad, sad story! Poor soul! Poor, forlorn, tortured soul! How glad she must have been to go! Aunt Faith—"

"Yes, dear Margaret!"

"Oh, nothing,—only—it seems dreadful sometimes, to feel that terrible things may be coming, coming toward one, and that one never can look forward, never know when they may come! I sometimes think, if I could see a year ahead, or even a week,—but one never knows. I suppose it is best, or it would not be!"

"Assuredly, dear child! When you think a little more, you will see the wisdom and the mercy of it. How could we go steadfastly along our path of every day, if some day we saw a pit at the farther end? Life would be impossible, Margaret."

"Yes, I—I suppose so!" said Margaret thoughtfully.

"And all the time," Mrs. Cheriton went on, "all the time, during the clear, calm days and years, my child, we are, or we ought to be, laying by, as it were; storing up light and strength and happiness for the dark days when we may so deeply need them. Think a moment! Think of all the happy days and years with your father! They are blessed memories, are they not, Margaret? every day is like a jewel that you take out and look at, and then put back in its case; you never lose these precious things that are all your own!"

"Oh, never! oh, how well you know, Aunt Faith! how you must have felt it all!" The girl raised her head, and saw the face of the aged woman transfigured with light and beauty. She also was looking back through the years,—who could tell how long!

"But suppose,"—it was still she who spoke,—"suppose now, Margaret, that these memories were other than they are! Suppose that instead of the blessed golden days, you had days of storm and anger and disagreement to look back on; that there had been unkindness on one side, unfaithfulness on the other; suppose it had been with you and your father as it has been with some parents and children that I have known,—how then?"

"Oh!" murmured Margaret, her eyes filling with tears, that yet had no bitterness in them; "but it could not have been so, Aunt Faith. Papa was an angel, you know; an angel of goodness and love."

"Now you see what I mean by storing up light against the dark days," said Mrs. Cheriton. "If he had not been loving and good,— and if you, too, had not been a good and dear daughter,—think what your possessions would be to-day. As it is, you have what can never be taken from you; and so if we go on steadfastly, as I said, content not to see before us, but cherishing and making the best of what we have to-day, the best of what to-day holds will be ours forever, till death comes to end all the partings and all the sorrow."

The last words were spoken rather to herself than to Margaret. The latter sat still, not daring to speak; for it seemed as if some beautiful vision were passing before the eyes of the old woman. She sat looking a little upward, with her lips slightly parted, the breath coming and going so softly that one could not perceive it, her hands clasped in her lap. Now the lips moved, and Margaret heard the low words of a prayer, rather breathed than whispered. Another moment, and the brown eyes grew bright and smiling once more, and the kindly gaze fell on the girl, who sat awestruck, half afraid to breathe.

"My poor Margaret!" said Mrs. Cheriton quickly. "My poor little girl, I have frightened you. Dear, when one is so old as I am the veil seems very thin, and I often look half through it and feel the air from the other side. But you—you must not stay here too long, you must not be saddened by an old woman's moods. You love to stay, and I love to have you, but it must not be too long. I will just tell you about the change in the rooms, and then—well, the Black Rooms remained shut up for many, many years after Aunt Phoebe's death. Indeed, I fancy they were never used until after your grandfather's death, when the property was divided, and your Uncle John took Fernley as his share. Then one of the first things he did was to throw open these rooms, send for a painter, and have them painted white from floor to ceiling, as you see. He had no use for them at that time, but he has told me that he did not like to be in the same house with anything black. Everything burnable was burned,—for your grandfather, as long as he lived, kept Aunt Phoebe's belongings just as she left them,—the brown crockery was smashed—"

"Oh, that was a pity!" cried Margaret. "Just for the curiosity—"

"I have a piece, my dear!" said Mrs. Cheriton. "Elizabeth Wilson—good Elizabeth—saved a piece for me; and she kept one of the black silk gowns (she has been in the house ever since she was a child), to put in the family chest. So there, Margaret, you have the story of Aunt Phoebe from beginning to end. And now you must go out and play."

"Oh, just a moment!" pleaded Margaret. "Aunt Faith,—Uncle John must be very nice."

"My dear, he is the best man in the world. There is not a doubt about it."

"Shall we see him at all, Aunt Faith?"

"You shall see him. I cannot say exactly when, but you shall see him, Margaret; that I promise you on the word of a centenarian. Now will you go, or shall Janet—"

"Oh, I will go! I will go! Good-bye, dear Aunt Faith. I have had the most delightful hour," and Janet came and closed the white door softly after her.

CHAPTER XI

HEROES AND HEROINES

"Oh for a knight like Bayard,
Without reproach or fear!"

"How to support life on such a day as this?" demanded Rita, coming out of her room, and confronting her cousins as they came upstairs. She had been asleep, and her dark eyes were still misty and vague. The others, on the contrary, had been running in the rain, and they were all a-tingle with life and fresh air, and a-twinkle with rain-drops. The moment was not a good one, and Rita's straight brows drew together ominously.

"You have been—amusing yourselves, it appears," she said, in the old withering tone that they were learning to forget. "Of course, here nothing matters; one may as well be a savage as an élégante in the wilderness; but I should be sorry to meet you in Havana, my cousins!"

Peggy hung her head, and tried to keep her muddy feet out of sight. Margaret only laughed, and held up her petticoats higher.

"You ought to have been with us, Rita!" she said. "We have had great fun. The garden is one great shower-bath, and the brook is roaring like a baby lion. I am really beginning to learn how to walk in wet feet, am I not, Peggy? I used to think I should die if my feet were wet. It is really delightful to feel the water go 'plop!' in and out of one's boots. Now, my dear," she added, "I really cannot let you be cross, because Peggy and I are in the most delightful good humour, and we came in on purpose, because we thought you would be awake, and would want to be amused. If you frown, Rita, I shall kiss you, all dripping wet, and you know you could not bear that."

She advanced, holding up her rosy, shining face, down which the drops were still streaming. Rita uttered a shriek and vanished.

"I don't see how you can talk to her that way," said Peggy admiringly. "When she opens her eyes at me, and pulls her eyebrows together, I feel about two inches high and three years old. You are brave in your own way, Margaret, if you can't pull people out of bogs."

Margaret laughed again. "My dear, I found it was the only way," she said. "If I let her ride over me—" Here she stopped suddenly, and with a change of tone bade Peggy hasten to change her wet clothes. "It is all very fine to get wet," she said, "and I am grateful for the lesson, Peggy; but I know that one must change when she comes in."

Peggy made a grimace, and said that at home she was often wet through from morning till night, and nobody cared; but Margaret resolutely pushed her into her room and shut the door, before going on to her own.

In a few minutes both girls, dry and freshly clad, knocked at Rita's door; and though her "Come in" still sounded rather sullen, it was yet a distinct invitation, and they entered. Rita had made this room over in her own way, much to Elizabeth's inconvenience. The chintz curtains were almost covered with little flags, emblems, feathery grasses, and the like, pinned here and there in picturesque confusion. A large Cuban flag draped the mantelpiece, and portraits of the Cuban leaders adorned the walls. Over the dressing-table was the great scarlet fan which had played such a conspicuous part in the drama of "Cuba Libre," and it was pinned to the wall with a dagger of splendid and alarming appearance. The mirror was completely framed in photographs, mostly of dark-eyed señoritas in somewhat exaggerated toilets. Inscriptions in every variety of sprawling hand testified to the undying love of Conchita, Dolores, Manuela, and a dozen others, for their all-beautiful Margarita, to part from whom was death.

If this were literally true, the youthful population of Cuba must have been sensibly diminished by Rita's departure. There were black-browed youths, too, some gazing tenderly, some scowling fiercely, all wearing the Cuban ribbon with all possible ostentation. One of these youths was manifestly Carlos Montfort, Rita's brother, for they were like enough to have been twins; another had been pointed out to Margaret, in a whisper charged with dramatic meaning, as "Fernando," the cousin on her mother's side, the handsomest man in Havana, and the most fascinating. Margaret looked coolly enough at this devastator of hearts, and thought that her own cousin Carlos was far handsomer. Peggy thought so, too; indeed, her susceptible sixteen-year-old heart was deeply impressed by Cousin Carlos's appearance, and she would often steal into the room during Rita's absence, to peep and sigh at the delicate, high-bred face, with its flashing dark eyes, and the hair that grew low on the forehead, with just the same tendril curls that made Rita's hair so lovely. Oh! Peggy would think, if her own hair were only dark, or even brown,—anything but this disgusting, wishy-washy flaxen. She had longed for dark eyes and hair ever since she could remember. Poor Peggy! But she kept her little romance to herself, and indeed it was a very harmless one, and helped her a good deal about keeping her hair neat and her shoe-strings tied.

When the girls went in now, they found Rita curled up on her sofa, with the robe and pillow of chinchilla fur that had come with her from Cuba. It was a bad sign, Margaret had learned, when the furs came out in warm weather. It meant a headache generally, and at any rate a chilly state of body, which was apt to be accompanied by a peevish state of mind. Still, she looked so pretty, peeping out of the soft gray nest! She was such a child, after all, in spite of her seventeen years,—decidedly, she must be amused.

"Well," said Rita, half dolefully, half crossly, "I cannot command solitude, it appears. I am desolated; I desire to die, while this frightful rain pours down, but I cannot die alone; that is not suffered me."

"Certainly not," replied Margaret cheerfully. "Don't die yet, please, dear, but when you feel that you must, we will be at hand to take your last wishes, won't we, Peggy?"

But Peggy thought Margaret cruel, and could only look at Rita remorsefully, feeling that she had sinned, she knew not how.

"And how are we to amuse ourselves?" added Margaret, seating herself on the couch at Rita's feet. "I think we must tell stories; it is a perfect day for stories. Oh, Peggy, don't you want to get my knitting, like the dear good child you are? I cannot listen well unless I have my knitting."

Peggy brought the great pink and gray blanket which had been Margaret's friend and companion for several months, and with it her own diminutive piece of work, a doily that she was supposed to be embroidering. Rita lay watching them with bright eyes, her eyebrows still nearer together than was desirable. At last, "Well," she said again. There was impatience and irritation in the tone, but there was interest, too.

"Well," replied Margaret, "I was only thinking what would be pleasantest to do; there are so many things. How would it do for each of us to tell a story,—a heroic story, such as will stand the rain, and not be afraid of a wetting?"

"Of our own deeds?" inquired Rita.

"Oh, perhaps hardly that. If I waited to find a heroic deed of my own performance, you might get tired, my dear. Somehow heroics do not come every day, as they used in story times. But I can tell you one of my father. Will you hear it?"

Rita nodded languidly; Peggy looked up eagerly.

"It was in the great Blankton fire," said Margaret.

"I don't suppose you know about it, Rita, but Peggy may have heard. No? Well, the country is very big, after all. It seems as if all the world must have heard of that fire. I was hardly more than a baby at the time, but I remember seeing the red glare, and thinking that we were not going to have any night that time, as the sun was getting up again as soon as he had gone to bed. We were living in Blankton that winter, for papa had some work that made it necessary for him to be near the Blankton libraries; Historical Society work, you know, as so much of his work was." She paused for some appreciative word, but none came. Apparently neither of her cousins had heard of the Historical Society, which had played so large a part in her father's life and her own.

"The whole sky was like blood!" she went on; "and when the smoke-clouds that hung low over the city blew aside, we could see the flames darting up, high, high, like pillars and spires. Oh! it was a beautiful, dreadful sight! I watched it, baby as I was, with delight. I never thought that my own father was in all that terrible glow and furnace, and that he came near losing his precious life to save another's."

"How?" cried Peggy, roused at the mention of saving life. "Did he start another fire to meet it?"

"Oh, no, no!" cried Margaret, in her turn failing to appreciate the Western point of view. "He tried to help put it out at first in the building where he was, and when he saw that was impossible, he went to work getting out his books and papers. They were very, very valuable; no money could have bought some of them, he said, for they were original documents, and in some cases there were no duplicates. They were Papa's treasures,—more to him than twenty fortunes. So he began taking them out, slowly and carefully, thinking he had plenty of time. But after he had taken out the first load, he heard cries and groans in a room near his own office, and going in, he found an old man, a wretched old miser that lived there all alone, in dirt and misery, though every one knew he was immensely rich. He seemed to have gone out of his mind with fright, and there he sat, his hands full of notes and bonds and things, screaming and crying, and saying that he could not go out, for he would be robbed, and he must stay there and burn to death. Papa tried to reason with him, but he would not listen, only screamed louder, and called Papa a robber when he tried to take the papers from him. Then Papa called to the men who were passing by to help him, but they were all so busy saving their own things, they could not stop, I suppose, or at any rate, they did not; and all the time the fire was coming nearer, and the smoke was getting thicker and thicker. Somebody who knew Papa called to him that the fire had reached his entry, and that in five minutes his office would be in flames. He started to run, thinking he could get out a few precious books, and let the others go while he got the old man out; but this time the poor old soul clung to him, and begged not to be left to burn, and looking out into the hall, Papa saw the smoke-cloud all shot with flame, and bright tongues licking along the walls toward him. So he took the old man by the arm and tried to lead him out, but he screamed that his box must go too, his precious box, or he should die of grief. That was his strong-box, and it was too heavy for him to lift, so he sat down beside it, hugging it, and saying that he would never leave it. Poor Papa was at his wit's end, for at any moment they might be surrounded and cut off from the stairs. So he heaved up the box and threw it out of the window, and then he took the old miser on his back and ran for his life. Oh, girls, there was only just time! He had to run through the fire, and his hair and beard were singed, and his clothes; but he got through, half blinded and choked, and almost strangled, too, for the old miser was clutching his throat all the time, and screaming out that he had murdered him."

"Why did he not drop him?" inquired Rita. "My faith, why should he be saved, the old vegetable?"

"Oh, Rita, you don't know what you are saying. It was a human life, and of course he had to save it; but it did seem cruel that the precious books and papers had to be sacrificed for just wretched money. That was the heroic part of it,—Papa's leaving the things that meant more to him than anything in the world, except me and his friends, and saving the old miser's money."

"If he could have saved him and the books, and let the money go to Jericho!" said Peggy; "but I suppose he couldn't."

"That was just it! The man was really out of his mind, you see, and if Papa had left him he might have run into the fire, or jumped out of the window, or done any other crazy thing. Well, that is my story, girls. Who shall come next,—you, Rita?"

Rita had been only partly roused by the story of the fire. An uncle saving a dirty old man and his money did not specially appeal to her; the hero should have been young and ardent, and should have saved a lady from the burning house. Peggy wanted to be responsive, but it seemed a great fuss to make over musty old books and papers; probably they were like those that Margaret made such a time about in the library here; Peggy had looked at some of them, and they were as dry as dry could be. If he had saved a dog, now, or a child,—and at the thought her eyes brightened.

"Do heroines count," she asked; "or must it be a man?"

"Of course they count!" cried Margaret, bending over her work to hide the tears that came to her eyes. She felt the glow checked in her heart,—knew that her story, her beloved story, had not struck the note that always thrilled her when she saw in thought her father, slender, gray-haired, carrying out the strange man, and leaving behind him, without a word, the fruits of years of toil.

"Of course heroines count, my dear! Have you one for us?"

"Ma did something nice once," said Peggy shyly; "she saved my life when I was a baby."

"Tell us!" cried both girls, and Rita's eyes brightened, for this seemed to promise better.

"It was when Pa first took up the claim," said Peggy. "The country was pretty wild then,—Indians about, and a good many big beasts: panthers, and mountain lions, and so on. I was the only girl, and I was two years old. Pa used to be out on the claim all day, and the boys with him, all except Hugh, and he was in bed at that time; and Ma used to work in the garden, and keep me by her so that I wouldn't get into mischief.

"One day she was picking currants, and I had been sitting by her, playing with some hollyhock flowers she had given me. She did not notice when I crawled away, but suddenly she heard me give a queer sort of scream. She turned round, and there was a big panther dragging me off down the garden path by my dress. Ma felt as if she was dead for a minute; but then she ran back to the seed-house—it was only a few steps off—and got a hoe that she knew was there, and tore off after the panther. It wasn't going very fast, for I was a pretty heavy baby, and it didn't know at first that any one was after it. When it heard Ma coming it started off quicker, and had almost got to the woods when she caught up. Ma raised that hoe and brought it down on the beast's head as hard as she knew how. It dropped me, and turned on her, grinning and snarling, and curling its claws all ready for a spring. She never stopped to draw breath; she raised the hoe again, and that time, she says, she prayed to the swing of it; and she brought it down, and heard the creature's skull go crash under it, and felt the hoe sink in. The panther gave a scream and rolled over, and then Ma rolled over too; and when Pa came home to dinner, a few minutes later, they were both lying there still, and I was trying to pick up my hollyhock flowers. We have never had hollyhocks since then; Ma can't bear 'em."

There was no doubt about the effect of Peggy's story. Before it was finished Rita was sitting bolt upright, her chinchilla robe thrown back, her hands clasped over her knee, her eyes alight with interest; and Margaret cried, "Oh, Peggy, Peggy, what a splendid story!"

"Well, it's true!" said Peggy.

"Of course it is; that's the splendid part. Oh, I am so proud to have an aunt so brave and strong. Aunt—why, Peggy, you have never told me your mother's name!"

"You never asked," said Peggy. "Her name is Susan."

Margaret blushed, and mentally applied the scourge to herself. It was true; she never had asked. Peggy had said that her mother had no education, and had got along very well without it; this was all that Margaret wanted to know. A shallow, ignorant woman, who had let her child grow up in such ignorance as Peggy's; and now she learned, all in a moment, of a strong, brave woman, helping her husband to clear the waste where their home was to be, making that home, bringing up her great family in love and rude plenty, and killing wild beasts with her own hard, honest hand. Margaret was learning a good deal this summer, and this was one of the most salutary lessons. She bowed her head and accepted it, but she only said aloud:

"Aunt Susan! I hope I shall know her some day. I shall put her in my heroine book, Peggy, from this minute." And the tone was so warm and hearty that Peggy's eyes filled with tears, and she felt dimly that she, too, had been neglectful of "Ma" of late, and resolved to write a good long letter that very afternoon.

"And now it is your turn, Rita!" said Margaret. "I give you till I knit to the end of this row to find a hero or heroine in your family. You must have plenty of them."

Rita laughed, and curled herself into another graceful, sinuous attitude. Her eyes shone. "My brother Carlos is in the mountains," she said; "my cousin Fernando with him. Pouf! if I were with them!"

She was silent a moment, and then went on, speaking slowly, and pausing every few minutes to blow little holes in her chinchilla robe, a favourite amusement of hers.

"The San Reals have plenty of heroes, heroines too; my mother was a San Real, you remember. What will you have, Marguerite? Far back, an ancestor of mine was the most beautiful woman in Spain. Her lover was seized by the Inquisition; she went to the Tribunal, accused herself, and died in his place. Will you have her for a heroine? My great-grandfather—he was a Grandee of Spain. The nephew of the king insulted him to the death, and thought his rank made him safe. He was found dead the next morning, and my great-grandfather lay dead beside him, with the dagger in his heart that had first slain the prince. Is he a hero such as you love, Marguerite?"

"No, not at all!" cried Margaret, "Rita, what dreadful tales! Those were the dark days, when people did not know better; but surely you must have some ancestors who were not murd—who did not die violent deaths."

"They are San Reals!" said Rita. "They had royal blood of Spain in their veins. Cold, thin, Northern blood cannot warm to true heroism." She sulked for some time after this, and refused to say anything more; but desire of imparting was strong in her, and Margaret's smile could not be resisted indefinitely.

"Come!" she said. "You meant no harm, Marguerite; you cannot understand me or my people, but I should have known it, and your birth is not your fault. Listen, then, and see if this will please you."

She seemed to meditate for some time, and when she spoke again it was still more slowly, as if she were choosing her words.

"Once on a time,—no matter when,—there was a war. A cruel, unjust, devilish war, when the people of—when my people were ground to the earth, tortured, annihilated. All that was right and true and good was on one side; on the other, all that was base and brutal and horrible. There was no good, none! they are—they were devils, allowed to come to earth,—who can tell why?

"The—the army of my people had suffered; they were in need of many things, of food, of shoes, but most of all of arms. The whole nation cried for bloodshed, and there were not arms for the half of them. How to get weapons? Near by there was another country, but a short way across the water—"

"Africa?" asked Peggy innocently. But Rita flashed at her with eyes and teeth.

"If you will be silent, Caliban! Do I tell this story, or do you? have I mentioned a name?"

"I beg pardon!" muttered poor Peggy. "I didn't mean to interrupt, Rita; I only thought Africa was the nearest to Spain across the water."

Rita glowered at her, and continued. "This neighbour-country was rich, great, powerful; but her people were greedy, slothful, asleep. They had arms, they had food, money, everything. Did they help my people in their need? I tell you, no!"

She almost shrieked the last words, and Margaret looked up in some alarm, but concluding that Rita was merely working herself up to a dramatic crisis, she went on with her knitting.

"To this rich, slothful country," Rita went on, dwelling on every adjective with infinite relish, "came a girl, a daughter of the country that was bleeding, dying. She was young; she had fire in her veins instead of blood; she was a San Real. She stayed in a house—a place—near the seashore, a house empty for the great part; full of rooms, empty of persons. The thought came to her,—Here I could conceal arms, could preserve them for my country, could deliver them to vessels coming by sea. It is a night expedition, it is a little daring, a little valour, the risk of my life,—what is that? I could arm my country, my brothers, against the tyrants. I could—" Rita paused, and both girls looked at her in amazement. She had risen from the couch, and now stood in the middle of the room; her slender form quivered with emotion; her great eyes shone with dark fire; her voice vibrated on their ears with new and powerful cadences.

"This girl—was alone. She needed help. With her in the house were others, her friends, but knowing little of her heart. Their blood flowed slowly, coldly; they were good, they were kind, but—would they help her? Would they brave danger for her sake, for the sake of the country that was dearer to her than life? Alone she was but one, with their aid—

"Listen! there came one day a letter to this house by the sea; it was for—for the person of whom I speak. Her brother was near, in a city not far off. He had come to collect arms, he had bought them, he must find a place to conceal them. Her dream was about to come true. She turned to her friends, the two whom she loved! She opened her arms, she opened her soul; she cried to them—"

"Stop!" said Margaret. She, too, had risen to her feet, and her face was very pale. Peggy looked from one to the other in alarm. Were they going to quarrel? Margaret's eyes were as bright as Rita's, but their light was calm and penetrating, not flashing and glowing with passion.

"Rita," she said, "I hope—I trust I am entirely wrong in what I cannot help thinking. I trust this is a story, and nothing else. It cannot be anything else!" she continued, her voice gaining firmness as she went on. "We are here in our uncle's house. He is away, he has left us in charge, having confidence in his brothers' daughters. If—if anything—if anybody should plan such a thing as you suggest, it would not only be ungrateful, it would be base. I could not harbour such a thought for an instant. Oh, I hope I wrong you! I hope it was only a dramatic fancy. Tell me that it was, my dear, and I will beg your pardon most humbly."

She paused for an answer, but Rita made none for the moment.

She stood silent, the very soul of passion, her eyes dilating, her lips apart, her breast heaving with the furious words that her will would not suffer to escape. Margaret almost thought she would spring upon her, like the wild creature she seemed. But presently a change came over the Cuban girl. A veil gathered over the glowing eyes; her hands unclenched themselves, opened softly; her whole frame seemed to relax its tension, and in another moment she dropped on her couch with a low laugh.

"Chère Marguerite," she said, "you, too, were born for the stage. Your climax, it was magnificent, très chère; pity that you spoiled it with an anti-climax." And she shrugged her shoulders. "My poor little story! You would not even let me finish it. No matter; perhaps it has no end; perhaps I was but trying to see if I could put life into you, statues that you are. Ah, it was a pretty story, if I could have been permitted to finish it!"

Margaret turned scarlet. "My dear, if I have been rude," she said, "I am very sorry, Rita; I thought—"

"You thought!" said Rita, her full voice dropping the words scornfully, in a way that was hard to bear. "Your thoughts are very valuable, très chère; I must not claim too many of them; they would be wasted on a poor patriot like me. And thou, Peggy, how didst thou like my story, eh?"

Rita turned so suddenly on Peggy that the poor child had not time to shut her mouth, which had been open in sheer amazement.

"Shut it!" said Rita sharply. "Is it a whale, or the Gulf of Mexico? I asked how you like my story, little stupid. Have you had sense to attend to it?"

Peggy's eyes filled with tears. A month ago she would have answered angrily, but now Rita was her goddess, and she could only weep at a harsh word from her.

"I—I think it is fine for a story, Rita," she answered slowly. "I loved to hear it. But—" Her blue eyes wandered helplessly for a moment, then met Margaret's steady gaze, and settled. "But if such a thing were true, Margaret would be right, wouldn't she?"

"And if you removed yourselves now?" queried Rita, turning her back to them with a sudden fling of the fur robe over her shoulder. "One must sleep in this place, or be talked to death, it appears. I choose sleep. My ears ring at present as with the sound of the sea,— a sea of cold babble! Adios, Señorita Calibana, Doña Fish-blood! I pray for relief!"

Margaret took Peggy's hand without a word, and they went out; but Peggy cried till dinner-time, and would not be comforted.

CHAPTER XII

IN THE SADDLE

"To witch the world with noble horsemanship."

Rita's "story" was not the first thing to rouse suspicion in Margaret's mind. It was rather the concluding word of a sentence that had been forming in her mind during the last ten days.

Something was on foot; some mystery hung about; she had felt thus much, and had felt, too, that it was connected with Rita; but all had been vague, uncertain.

Rita had been receiving many letters with the New York postmark; but what of that? It was not Margaret's business to take notice of her cousin's letters. She had met Rita once or twice at the foot of the garret stairs, evidently returning from a visit to that place of shadowy delight. What of that? Rita had said each time that she had been looking for such and such a costume; that she was planning a charade, a new tableau, that would be sure to ravish her cousins; and in the evening she would produce the charade or the tableau, and sure enough, it would be enchanting, and they were delighted, and most grateful to her for the pains she took to amuse them. And yet—and yet—had she been at these pains until lately? Had not Margaret herself been the one who must think of the evening's amusement, plan the game, the reading, or singing, which should keep the three various natures in harmonious accord? So it had surely been, until these last ten days; and now—

But how hateful to suspect, when it might be that Rita was merely feeling that perhaps she had not done her share, and had realised that with her great talent and her lovely voice and presence, she was the one to plan and execute their little entertainments? And what should Margaret suspect? It was not her nature to be anything but trustful of those around her; and yet—and yet—

But now her suspicions had taken definite shape, and Rita herself had confirmed them. There could no longer be any doubt that she was planning to take advantage of their uncle's continued absence to aid her brother,—who was in New York, as Margaret knew, in spite of Rita's recent declaration that he was in the mountains,—and to conceal arms in Fernley House, and have them shipped from there. It seemed impossible; it seemed a thing out of a play or a novel, but she could not doubt the fact. After all, Rita was a person for a play or a novel. This thing, which to Margaret seemed unspeakable, was to Rita but a natural impulse of patriotism, a piece of heroism.

Of course she would not be able to do it; no person in her senses would attempt such a thing, on Long Island, only a few miles from New York; but the hot-blooded young Cubans would not realise that, and they might make some attempt which, though futile, would bring disagreeable consequences to Mr. Montfort and to all concerned. What was Margaret to do? The absurdity of the whole thing presented itself to her keenly, and she would have been glad enough to turn it all into a jest, and take it as the "story" with which Rita had tried to rouse her cool-blooded cousins; but that could not be. Rita had meant every word she said, and more; that was evident. What was Margaret to do? Her first thought was of Mrs. Cheriton; her second of John Strong, the gardener. Aunt Faith ought not, she was sure, to be disturbed or made anxious; her hold on life was too slender; her days must flow evenly and peacefully, as Uncle John had arranged them for her; it would never do to tell her of this threatened, fantastic danger. But John Strong! he was Mr. Montfort's confidential servant, almost his friend. Nay, Aunt Faith had spoken of him as "a good friend," simply and earnestly. He knew Uncle John's address, no doubt; he would give it to her, or write himself, as seemed best. It was dreadful to betray her cousin, but these were not the days of melodrama, and it was quite clear that Fernley House could not be made a deposit of arms for the Cuban insurgents during its master's absence. So with a clear conscience, though a heavy heart, Margaret sought the garden.

John Strong was there, as he always was in the morning, fondling his roses, clipping, pruning, tying up, and setting out. In the afternoons he was never visible. Margaret had heard his voice occasionally in Mrs. Cheriton's rooms, but had never seen him there; he had evidently other work, or other haunts of his own, which kept him out of the way. She could not help knowing that he used her uncle's private sitting-room, but she took it for granted that it was with Mr. Montfort's leave and for his business. Rita might mistrust this man; but no one of Northern blood could look on the strong, quiet face without feeling that it was that of one of nature's noblemen, at least.

"John," said Margaret, after she had admired the roses and listened to a brief but eloquent dissertation upon Catherine Mermet and Maréchal Niel, "how near are we to the sea?"

"To the sea, Miss Margaret? Call it a quarter of a mile. The rise of the land hides it from Fernley, but you will notice that we are near, by the sound of it; and you have been down to the shore a number of times, I think."

"Yes; oh, yes! I know it is very near. I was only thinking—John, would it be easy for—persons—to come here from the shore, without being seen? I mean, could a vessel lie off here and not attract attention?"

John Strong looked at her keenly. "That depends, Miss," he said. "By day, no; by night, yes. It is a quiet part of the shore, you see."

"Do you know when Mr. Montfort is coming home?" was Margaret's next question; and as she put it she looked straight into the gardener's brown eyes, and they looked straight into hers. She fancied that John Strong changed colour a little.

"I have not heard from him lately," he said quietly. "I think he will be here very soon now. Could I—may I ask if anything is distressing you, my—Miss Margaret?"

Margaret hesitated. The temptation was strong upon her to tell the whole tale to this man, whom she felt she could trust entirely; but the thought of Rita held her back. She would say what was necessary, and no more.

"I—I think—" she began timidly, "it might be well for you to be watchful at night, John. The Cubans—I have heard rumours—there might be vessels,—do you think, possibly—"

She broke off. The whole thing seemed like a nursery nightmare, impossible to put into plain English without exposing its absurdity. But John Strong glanced at her again, and his eyes were grave.

"Miss Rita is deeply interested in the Cuban war, I believe," he said, with meaning.

Margaret started. "How did you know?" she asked. "Surely she has not—"

John Strong laughed. "Hardly," he said. "Miss Rita does not converse with menials. It was Peggy—Miss Peggy, I should say—who told me about it. She was quite inclined to take fire herself, but I think I cooled her down a bit. These are dangerous matters for young ladies to meddle with. I think she told me that young Mr. Carlos Montfort was now in New York?"

"I—I believe so," said Margaret. She was angry with Peggy for talking so freely, yet it was a great help to her now, for John Strong evidently understood more of the matter than she would have liked to tell him.

"You may trust me, Miss Margaret, I think," he said presently, after a few moments of silent snipping. "It is not necessary for me to know anything in particular, even if there is anything to know. I am an old soldier, and used to keeping watch, and sleeping with one eye open. You may trust me. You have said nothing of this to Mrs. Cheriton?" He looked up quickly.

"No; I thought she ought not to be distressed—"

"That was right; that was very right. You have shown—that is, you may depend on me, young lady. May I cut this bud for you? It is a perfect one, if I may say so. Perhaps you will look closer at it, Miss; (Miss Rita is observing you from the balcony, and you would not wish)—there, Miss. I shall bring some cut flowers into the dining-room later, for arrangement, as you ask. Good morning, Miss."

Margaret returned to the house, half relieved, half bewildered. John Strong was certainly a remarkable person. She did not understand his position here, which seemed far removed from that of a domestic, but after all, it was none of her business. And even if he did speak of Peggy by her first name, was it Margaret's place to reprove him? He was almost old enough to be Peggy's grandfather.

Rita had apparently forgotten the storm of the day before. She was in high good humour, and greeted Margaret with effusion.

"Just in time, Marguerite. Where have you been? We have called till we are hoarse. Look at us; we go to ride. We are to have an exhibition of skill, on the back of the white beast. Behold our costumes, found in the garret."

Margaret looked, and laughed and admired. Rita was dressed in a long black velvet riding-habit, with gold buttons, a regal garment in its time, but now somewhat rubbed and worn; a tall hat of antique form perched upon her heavy braids, and she looked very businesslike. Peggy had found no such splendour, but had put on a scarlet military coat over her own bicycle skirt. "Finery is good," she said, "but not on horseback." A three-cornered hat, with the mouldering remains of a feather, completed her costume, and she announced herself as the gentleman of the party.

"Rita was saying what a pity it was there were no boys here, and I told her I ought to have been a boy, and I would do my best now," said Peggy good-naturedly. Rita made a little grimace, as if this were not the kind of boy she desired, but she nodded kindly at Peggy, and said she was "fine."

"And you, Marguerite? How will you appear? Will you find a cap and spectacles, and come as our grandmother? That would approve itself, n'est-ce-pas?" It was laughingly said, but the sting was there, nevertheless, and was meant to be felt.

"Oh, I should delay you," replied Margaret. "Let me come as I am, and be ringmaster, or audience, or whatever you like. I never rode in my life, you know." Peggy opened wide her eyes, Rita curled her lip, but Margaret only laughed. "Frightful, isn't it? but how would you have me ride in my father's study? And the horses that went by our windows had mostly drays behind them, so they were not very tempting. Is William going to saddle White Eagle for you, girls?"

"William has gone to the mill, or to bed, or somewhere," said Peggy. "I am going to saddle him myself. John Strong said I might."

They went out to the great, pleasant barn, and while Peggy saddled the good horse, Rita and

Margaret mounted the old swing, and went flying backward and forward between the great banks of fragrant hay.

"Isn't it good to be a swallow?" said Margaret. "I wonder if we shall really fly some day; it really seems as if we might."

"I would rather be an eagle," said Rita. "To flutter a little, here and there, and sleep in a barn,—that would not be a great life. An eagle, soaring over the field of battle,—aha! he is my bird! But what is this outcry? Has he bitten thee, Peggy?"

For Peggy was shouting from below; yet when they listened, the shouts were of wonder and delight.

"Oh, girls, do just look here! There is a new horse,—a colt! Oh, what a beauty!"

The girls came down hastily, and ran to the door of the second box stall, which had been empty since they came. There stood a noble young horse, jet black, with a single white mark on his forehead. His coat shone like satin, his eyes beamed with friendly inquiry.

Already Peggy had her head against his shoulder, and was murmuring admiration in his ear.

"You lovely, you dear, beautiful thing, where did you come from? Oh, Margaret, isn't he a darling? Come and see him!"

Margaret came in rather timidly; she was not used to animals, and the horse seemed very large, tramping about freely in his ample stall. But he received her so kindly, and put his nose in her pocket with such confiding grace, that her fears were soon conquered. Rita patted him graciously, but kept her distance. "Very fine, my dear, but the straw smells, and gets on one's clothes so. Saddle me this one, Peggy, and you can have the white one yourself."

"Are we—have we leave to take this horse?" asked Margaret, colouring. It was too horrid that she must always play the dragon,—as if she liked it,—and of course the others thought she did.

"Have we been forbidden to take the horse, dear?" asked Rita with dangerous sweetness. "No? But perhaps you were told to keep watch on us by your friend, the servant, who wears his master's clothes? Again, no? Then kindly permit me, at least, to do as I think best."

"Oh, Rita!" cried Peggy, "perhaps we ought not—"

"Chut!" cried Rita, flashing upon her in the way that always frightened Peggy out of her wits. "Do you saddle me the horse, or do I do it myself?"

Margaret thought it was highly improbable that Rita could do it herself, but she said no more. A difficulty arose, however. There was found to be but one saddle. "Never mind!" said Peggy. "I can ride bareback just as well as saddleback; but I am afraid, Rita—"

"Afraid!" cried Rita. "You too, Peggy? My faith, what a set!"

"Afraid the saddle will not fit the black!" said Peggy, looking for once defiantly at her terrible cousin. "White Eagle is so big, you see; the saddle was made for him, and it slips right off this fellow's back."

Rita fretted and stamped her pretty feet, and said various explosive things under her breath, and not so far under but that they could be heard pretty well, but all this did not avail to make the saddle smaller or the new horse bigger; so at last she was obliged to mount White

Eagle, and to have the mortification of seeing Peggy vault lightly on the back of the black beauty. He had never been ridden before, perhaps; certainly he was not used to it, for he reared upright, and a less practised horsewoman than Peggy would have been thrown in an instant; but she sat like a rock, and stroked the horse between his ears, and patted his neck, and somehow wheedled him down on his four legs again. Margaret watched with breathless interest. This was all new to her. Rita looked graceful and beautiful, and rode with ease and skill, but Peggy was mistress of the situation. The black horse flew here and there, rearing, squealing with excitement, occasionally indulging in something suspiciously like a "buck;" but Peggy, unruffled, still coaxed and caressed him, and showed him so plainly that she was there to stay as long as she felt inclined, that after a while he gave up the struggle, and settling down into a long, smooth gallop, bore her away like the wind over the meadow and up the slope that lay beyond. Now they came to a low stone wall, and the watchers thought they would turn back; but Peggy lifted the black at it, and he went over like a bird. Next moment they were out of sight over the brow of the hill.

"Oh," cried Margaret, turning to Rita, her face aglow with pleasure, "wasn't that beautiful? Why, I had no idea the child could ride like that, had you? I never knew what riding was before."

Rita tried to look contemptuous, but the look was not a success. "A gentlewoman does not require to ride like a stable-boy!" was all she said. She was evidently out of humour, so Margaret was silent, only watching the hill, to see when the pair would come galloping back over the brow.

Here they were! Peggy was waving her hand—her hat had flown off at the first caracole, and Rita had ridden over it several times—and shouting in jubilation. Her hair flew loose over her shoulders, her short skirt was blown about in every direction, but her eyes were so bright, her face so rosy and joyous, that she was a pleasant sight to see, as, leaping the fence, she came sweeping along over the meadow.

"Hail!" cried Margaret, when she came within hearing. "Hail, daughter of Chiron! gloriously ridden, O youthful Centauress!"

Peggy did not know who Chiron was, but she caught the approving sound of the words, and waved her hand. "Come on, Rita!" she cried. "Take the Eagle over the fence! It's great fun. I'm going to try standing up in a minute, when he is a little more used to me."

They set off at an easy gallop, and White Eagle took the fence well enough, though it was his first, and he was no colt, like the black. Then they circled round and round the meadow, sometimes neck and neck, sometimes one far in advance. Generally it was Peggy, for the black was far the swifter animal of the two; but now and then she pulled him in, like the good-natured girl she was, and let her cousin gallop ahead. Margaret watched them with delight, not a pang of envy disturbing her enjoyment. What a perfect thing it was! how enchanting to be one with your horse, and feel his strong being added to your own! How —

But what was this? All in a minute, something happened. The black put his foot in a hole,—a woodchuck's burrow,—stumbled, pitched forward, and threw Peggy heavily to the ground. He recovered himself in a moment, and stood trembling; but Peggy lay still. Margaret was at her side in an instant. The child had struck her head on a stone, and was insensible, and bleeding profusely from a cut on the left temple. Rita dismounted and came near.

"Some water, please!" said Margaret. "Bring water quickly, Rita, while I stop the bleeding. And give me your handkerchief, will you, before you go?" She held out one hand, which was already covered with blood; glancing up, she saw that Rita was pale as death, and trembling violently.

"What is it?" cried Margaret. "Are you hurt,—ill? hold her, then, and I will run."

"No,—no!" said Rita, shuddering. "It is—the blood! I cannot bear the sight. I will go—I will send Elizabeth. Is she dead, Margaret? It is too terrible!"

"Dead? no!" said Margaret vehemently.

"She is only stunned a little, and has cut her head. If I had some water, I could manage perfectly. Do go, Rita!"

Rita seemed hardly able to move. She was ghastly white; her eyes sought, yet avoided, the red stream which Margaret was checking with steady hand. She did, however, move toward the house; and at the same moment Margaret had the satisfaction of feeling Peggy move slightly. The blue eyes opened part way; the mouth twitched,—was Peggy giggling, even before she regained consciousness? Margaret bent over her anxiously, afraid of some shock to the brain. But now the eyes opened again, and it was Peggy's own self that was looking at her, and—yes! undoubtedly laughing.

"Don't be scared, Margaret," she said, speaking faintly, but with perfect command of her senses. "It isn't the first 'cropper' I have come; I shouldn't have minded at all, only for my head. But—I say, Margaret, didn't I hear Rita going on about blood, and asking if I was dead?"

"Yes, dear; she is evidently one of those people who faint at the sight of blood. And you do look rather dreadful, dear, though I don't mind you a bit. And you must not talk now; you truly must not!"

"Rubbish! I'm going to get up in a minute, as soon as the water comes. But—I say, Margaret, how about the Cuban war? Do you suppose—the rest of them—feel the same way about blood? because—"

"Peggy, I am surprised at you!" said Margaret. "Hush this moment, or I will let your head drop!"

CHAPTER XIII

IN THE NIGHT

> Quand on conspire, sans frayeur
> Il faut se faire conspirateur;
> Pour tout le monde il faut avoir
> Perruque blonde, et collet noir!"

Peggy's injury proved to be slight, as she herself had declared, but the jar had been considerable, and her head ached so that she was glad to be put to bed and nursed by Margaret. Rita hovered about, still very pale, and apparently much more disturbed by the accident than the actual sufferer. She put many questions: Would Peggy be well to-morrow? Probably still weak? Would it be necessary for her to remain in her room this evening? In that case, what would Margaret do? Would she leave her to Elizabeth's care, and come down as usual?

"Certainly not!" Margaret replied. "Elizabeth will stay with Peggy at tea-time, but otherwise I shall not leave her. You don't mind staying alone, Rita? Of course, there is not much to be done; Peggy is not ill at all, only weak and tired, but she likes to have me with her. You will not be lonely?"

No; Rita had letters to write. She should do very well. Desolated, of course, without the two who were her soul and her existence; but Margaret understood that she could not bear the sight of sickness; it had been thus from infancy. Margaret nodded kindly, and went back into Peggy's room, with an impression that Rita was pleased at having her out of the way. Out of the way of what? But Margaret could not think about mysteries now. Peggy wanted to talk, and to have her head stroked, and to know that Margaret was near her.

"Your hand is so smooth, Margaret. I never felt anything like it; and the smoothness and coolness seem to go into my head, and stop the aching. Do you think this is being sick? If it is, I like it."

Margaret saw that the child was excited, and her eyes were overbright. "No; this is not being sick," she said quietly. "But you ought to be sleepy by this time, my pussy. Lie still now, like a good child, and I will sing to you. Will you have the 'Bonny House o' Airlie?'"

But it was long before Peggy could be quieted. She wanted to talk. She was full of reminiscences of former "croppers" in the lives of the various members of her family. She wanted to tell how Jim was dragged by the buffalo bull he was taming; how Pa caught the young grizzly by his paws, and held him until George came with the rifle; how Brown Billy ran away with her when she was six years old, and how she held on by his mane till he lay down and rolled in the creek, and then swam ashore. Her brain was feverishly excited, and it was not till late in the evening that Margaret succeeded in singing and soothing the tired girl to sleep. At length Peggy lay still, and her thoughts began to sink away into soft dreams, lulled by the soft hand on her brow, and the smooth, sweet voice in her ears. She opened her eyes to say, "I love you, Margaret; I love you best, over and over, all the time. If I thought I didn't for a bit, that was just because I was a stupid, and she—but now I know." And Peggy smiled, and smiling, fell asleep.

Margaret sat still for a time, listening to the breathing that grew deeper and more regular as the minutes went on. She had brought her own bed across the hall, meaning to sleep with Peggy, in case of her waking in the night; though that was hardly likely. It was ten o'clock now, and Rita was probably asleep. She would go down for a moment to see that all was well, and perhaps have a word with Elizabeth, if she were not gone to bed. She went softly to the door, and turned the handle noiselessly. The door was locked!

Greatly startled, Margaret stood motionless for a few minutes, thinking and listening. At first all was still. Footsteps above her head,—Elizabeth was going to bed; then the familiar creak of the good woman's bed; then silence again. Rita's room was across the hall, and she could hear no sound from there. Through the open window came the soft night noises: the dew dripping from the chestnut leaves, a little sleepy wind stirring the branches, a nut falling to the ground. How still!

Hark! did a twig snap then? Was some one moving through the shrubbery, brushing gently against the leaves? And then, as her heart stood still to listen, Margaret heard a low, musical whistle. She stole to the window, and standing in the shadow of the curtain, looked out. A light was burning in her room, and at first she could see nothing but blackness outside. Gradually, the outlines of the great chestnut stole out from the empty darkness, a hard black against the soft gloom of the night. Then the shrubbery behind; and then—was something moving there? Were those two figures standing by the tree?

The whistle was repeated; and now Margaret heard the swift rustle of silk brushing against her door, then fluttering from baluster to baluster, as Rita sped down the stairs. A door opening softly, and now three figures stood under the chestnut-tree. Words were whispered, greetings exchanged; then the three figures stole away into the blackness.

Margaret felt helpless for a moment. Locked in,—her cousin asleep here, exhausted if not ill, and needing absolute quiet,—and going on downstairs—what?

She must know! She must call John Strong, and warn him that her fears were realised, and that unwelcome visitors were already at the doors of Fernley, perhaps already within. But how was it possible? She ran to the window and looked down. Full twenty feet! To jump was impossible; even Peggy could not have done it. Peggy! yes! but Peggy could get out. Only the other night she had had a climbing frenzy, and had slid down the gutter-spout, half for the joy of it, half to tease Margaret, who was in terror till she reached the ground, and then in greater terror when the young gymnast came "shinning" up again, shouting and giggling. The spout! Margaret stood looking at it now. For a moment her courage deserted her, and she wrung her hands and began to sob under her breath; but this would not do! Her nerves knew the resolute shake of the shoulders, and shrank into obedience. She set her lips firmly, and there crept into her face a certain "dour" look that may have come from her Scottish ancestors. "If a thing has to be done, why, it must be done!" she said to herself. "Anyhow, there will be solid ground at the bottom, not a quaking bog."

Could she do it? She had never climbed in her life. She had been wont to grow dizzy on any great height; and here she reflected that she had inwardly laughed at Rita, a few hours before, for growing dizzy at the sight of blood. "But I have to learn so many lessons!" said poor Margaret, and with that she laid her hand on the spout. A moment longer she waited, but no longer in hesitation,—she was simply asking for strength from One who had never refused it yet; then she clasped the pipe with both hands, swung herself out as she had seen Peggy do, and slid down, down, down.

Her hands were torn and bleeding, but she reached the ground in safety, falling several feet, but escaping with a few bruises which she did not feel at the time. She ran round the house toward the east wing, where the gardener's room was, but stopped half-way. The door of the ground-floor room, her uncle's private room, was open; a light was burning inside. Possibly John Strong was himself on the watch, and she need go no farther. Margaret turned hastily, entered the room,—and was confronted by two young gentlemen in Spanish cloaks and broad-brimmed hats.

Margaret's first impulse was to run away; her second, to stand and wait, feeling that she was at a play, and that the next scene was going to be very thrilling; but the third impulse was the right one, and she stepped forward, holding out her hand.

"You are my Cousin Carlos, I am sure!" she said, addressing the taller of the two lads (for they were only lads, she saw to her unspeakable relief; the elder could not be more than twenty). "I am Margaret Montfort. You—you have seen Rita?"

Don Carlos Montfort gasped and bowed, hat in hand. He and his companion were evidently new to their rôle of conspirators, for they were piteously ill at ease, and their dark eyes roamed about as if in search of retreat; but he managed to say something about the distinguished honour—a spare hour to visit his sister—delight at making the acquaintance of a relative so charming,—here he stopped and looked over his shoulder, for footsteps were heard, and he hoped

Rita was coming. Already he and his comrade were cursing themselves for having been asses enough to be drawn into this scrape; why had they attended to a foolish girl instead of going their own way? Now they were in a trap—was that Rita coming?

The door of the secret staircase was open, showing which way the girl had gone. But the steps that were now descending were heavy, though quiet,—far different from the rush of an excited bird that had gone up a moment before Margaret's appearance. They were to follow Rita,—she went to light a candle. Ah! what was this?

The young men recoiled, and their dark eyes opened to their fullest width; Margaret's hands came together with a violent clasp. Down the narrow stair and into the room came a man in a black velvet jacket; a tall man, with bright, dark eyes and a grave face. He held a candle in his hand; he set it down, and turned to the two disconcerted Spaniards.

"My nephew," said Mr. Montfort, "I am glad to welcome you and your friend to Fernley House. I am your Uncle John!"

Margaret was not conscious of any surprise. It seemed part of the play, and as if she had known it all along, but had not been allowed to realise it, for some dramatic reason. She saw John Strong—John Montfort—shaking hands with the two unhappy young men, and trying to put them at their ease by speaking of the bad roads and the poor conveyances that were undoubtedly to blame for their arriving so late. She saw and heard, but still as in a dream. Her real thought was for Rita; what would she do? What desperate step might follow this disconcerting of her cherished plan?

Unconsciously Margaret had moved forward, till now she stood the nearest to the foot of the stairs. She looked up into the darkness, with some thought of going to her cousin, telling her gently what had happened, and quieting her so that she might come down and face the situation, and meet her uncle. All at once, from that darkness above, a bright light sprang up, and the same instant there rang out a wild and terrible shriek.

"Help! Carlos, help! I burn!"

The three men started forward, but they were not the first. Margaret was conscious of but a single movement as she flew up the stairs, never stumbling, lighted by that fearful glare above. To spring into the garret, to drag down the heavy old cloak—the same that once had frightened the three girls on their first visit—that hung close by the stairway, to fling herself upon Rita, throwing her down, muffling her, smothering and beating out the flames that were leaping up toward the girl's white, wild face,—all this was done in one breath, it seemed to her. She knew nothing in the world but the fire she was fighting, the little flames that, choked down in one place, came creeping out at her from another, playing a dreadful hide-and-seek among the folds of the cloak, starting up under her very hands; but Margaret caught them in her hands, and strangled the life out of them, and fought on. It was but a moment, in reality. Another second or two and the flames would have had the mastery; but Margaret's swift rush had been in time, and the good heavy cloak—oh, the blessed weight and closeness of its fabric!—had shut out the air, so that by the time the last of the three anxious pursuers had reached the garret, the fire was out, and only smoke and charred woollen remained to tell of the terrible danger. Only these—and the two hands, burned and blistered, that Margaret was holding out to her uncle, as he bent anxiously over her.

"Don't be angry with her, Uncle!" cried the girl. And she knew nothing more.

CHAPTER XIV

EXPLANATIONS

"And she really is not hurt, Uncle John?"

"Not so much as an eyelash! You were so quick, child! How did you manage it? She had only time to scream and put her hands to her face, before you were upon her. The thing that flared up so was a lace shawl she had on her arm,—switched it into the candle, of course!—and that she dropped. It is not of her I am thinking, but of you, my dear, brave Margaret!" He bent over her tenderly and anxiously; but she smiled brightly in his face.

"Truly, they hardly hurt at all! As you say, I must have been very quick, and the flames were only little ones. Elizabeth has bandaged them so beautifully; the pain is almost gone already."

They were in Margaret's room; she on her sofa, with her hands swathed in bandages, but otherwise looking quite her own self, only a little paler than usual; her uncle sitting by her, his hand on her arm. Peggy fluttered in and out of the room, entirely recovered from the effect of her fall the day before, and proud beyond measure of having charge of Margaret, who last night had been watching and tending her. Peggy's nursing was of doubtful quality; already she had baptised Margaret twice,—once with gruel, again with cologne, when the cork with which she had been struggling came out suddenly, deluging her patient with fragrance.

But her good will was so hearty, her affection so ardent and so anxious to prove itself, that Margaret had not the heart to deny her anything, and submitted to having her hair brushed in a style that was entirely new to her, and that made her wink at each vigorous stroke of the brush.

Rita had not been seen since the night before, save by Elizabeth, who pronounced her well, but "a little upset, Miss!" and Elizabeth's face was a study in repression as she spoke.

"And the boys, Uncle?" Margaret asked, when she was assured of Rita's safety. "What have you done with them?"

Mr. Montfort laughed.

"Poor boys!" he said. "Poor lads! they have had a hard time of it."

"Oh, do tell me!" cried Margaret.

"Why, they are all right; the boys are all right!" said Mr. Montfort. "It is that little monkey over there," nodding toward Rita's room, "who has made all the trouble. They have been fighting, it is true, and have been in the mountains with the insurgents. Very interesting their account of it is, too. If I were thirty years younger—but that is not the point. They were sent to New York by their chief on private business; something of importance, but perfectly legitimate,—nothing to do with arms or anything of the kind. Well, Carlos did not tell Rita the object of his coming, and she instantly saw fire and gunpowder, treason and plot,—in short, cooked up a whole melodrama to suit herself,—and believed it, I have no doubt, an hour after she invented it. She wrote Carlos mysterious letters, imploring him to come to her secretly; that her fate and that of her country depended upon his faithfulness and silence; that she was surrounded by spies—"

"Poor Peggy and me!" cried Margaret. "And you, too, Uncle John! She has really had painful suspicions of you."

"No doubt, no doubt! but in my case she had a right to suspicions. We will come to that presently. In short, the boy got the impression that his sister was immured in a kind of dungeon, surrounded by people who were unkind to her, and unable to get away or to call for help openly. He says he ought to have known better, for apparently she has been acting plays ever since she was short-coated; but this time he was really taken in, and came here last night, with his friend and cousin, meaning to rescue his sister and take her home to Cuba. Found her not desiring in the least to be rescued, but bent on hiding them both in the garret, and keeping them there till a cargo of arms and a vessel could be brought from New York. You know the rest. Carlos was in the library when I came up, waiting for an interview with Rita. I think it may be a lively one."

"And the other; the cousin? I hardly saw him. They were both so embarrassed, poor dears!"

"Seems a good little fellow; good little fellow enough! Gentlemanly boys, both of them. Carlos is much more of a person than the other. He—Fernando Sanchez—admires Rita a good deal, I should say, and tries to find her conduct admirable; but her brother—hark!"

Something like a silken whirlwind came rushing up the stairs and across the hall; something that sobbed with fury, and stamped with feet that were too small to make much noise; then a door on the other side of the hall shut with a bang that made the solid walls quiver. Margaret and her uncle looked at each other. Presently Peggy came in, with round, frightened eyes.

"What is the matter with Rita?" she asked. "Has she been in here? She came flying across the hall just now—oh, dear! I was just coming out of my room, and she took me and shook me, just as hard as she could shake. Why, my teeth chattered, Margaret! and then she flung off into her room, and slammed the

door. My! she was in a tantrum! Oh, I—I—beg your pardon!" She faltered at the sight of her uncle, and hung back. She had only learned this morning of the astonishing transformation of her friend the gardener into the unknown and formidable relative.

Mr. Montfort held out his hand, with the smile that always went to Peggy's heart.

"Well, Miss Peggy," he said, "and what roses will you have to-day? My dear child," he added, seeing that she was really distressed, "you are not really troubled at my little masquerade? I am going to tell you all about it soon,—as soon as I can see my three Margarets together. I feel that I owe you all an explanation. Margaret has already heard part of my story, and when Rita comes in, as I hope she will do soon,—I sent word to her that I should be glad to see her here when she had had her talk with her brother,—we will go over the whole matter, and find out what John Strong and John Montfort have to say for themselves."

He turned the subject, and began to talk of the garden and the flowers, in his usual quiet, cheerful way, till Peggy began to steal shy glances at him under her eyelashes, and finally to hold her head up and smile without looking as if she had stolen a sheep.

They had not long to wait. Before they had settled the position of the new rose-bed, Rita's door was heard to open softly; then came the sound of trailing garments in slow and stately motion, and the next moment Rita entered the room.

She was dressed in deep black from head to foot. A black veil covered her hair, and hung gracefully from her shoulders, and in her hand she carried a black fan.

There were dark circles under her eyes, and she looked pale but lovely. Mr. Montfort rose and came forward, holding out his hand. "My dear niece," he said with some formality, "let us shake hands in all friendliness."

But Rita did not take the outstretched hand. Instead, she folded her hands, and sank down in the deepest and most beautiful courtesy that ever was seen. Her eyes remained downcast, the long lashes resting on her clear, white cheek.

"My uncle," she said, and her tone was dignified, pathetic, and resentful, all in one, "I come to make my submission to you, and to ask your pardon for my offences. My brother demands it, and I obey the head of my house, the representative of my father. I pray you to forgive me!"

Mr. Montfort subdued an unruly twinkle in his eyes, and answered gravely:

"I pardon you, my niece, freely. I beg you to consider the matter as if it had never existed. My house is yours, and all that it contains; pray be seated."

Rita looked up, startled at hearing in English the phrase of Spanish courtesy so familiar to her ears; but Mr. Montfort's face was inscrutable, as he brought forward a chair, and handed her to it as if she were a duchess.

But Rita was not ready to sit down yet; she had arranged her scene, and must go through with it. She advanced, and knelt down by Margaret's couch. "Marguerite," she said sadly, "you saved my life. It was valueless, I have learned; it was not worth the saving; nevertheless I thank you from my heart of hearts. I—" Here she caught sight of the bandaged hands, which Margaret had been trying to conceal beneath the afghan. Instantly the tragic mask fell from Rita's face, and left a real human countenance, full of pity and anxiety. "My dear!" she cried. "My angel, my poor suffering Marguerite. Ah! you sent me word it was nothing. You are injured, terribly injured, and by my fault. Ah! now Carlos must let me die, as I desire. Life is no longer possible!"

The words were extravagant, but there was real grief and distress in the tone. She laid her head on Margaret's shoulder and sobbed aloud; and Peggy was heartily glad to hear her cry, and cried in sympathy. Margaret could not stroke the dark head, but she moved her own near it, and whispered little comforting words, and kissed the soft hair. And presently, finding that the sobs only increased in violence, she whispered to Rita that she was distressing her uncle, and that she really must try to be quiet on his account. At the sound of his name, Rita froze again, though not to her former degree of rigour; with a fervent kiss on Margaret's brow, she rose, and finally took the chair that had been placed for her. Mr. Montfort sat down opposite, and a brief silence followed. He seemed to be thinking what he should say. At length he spoke.

"My dear nieces, this is a day of explanations, and I feel that I owe you all an explanation of my conduct, which, doubtless, must appear strange to you. I—well, I suppose I am an eccentric man. I have always been considered so, and I confess not without apparent reason. I have often been able to justify to myself conduct which has seemed strange to others; and it has been my misfortune to live so much alone, that perhaps I may rely too much on this practice of self-justification.

"It is now five years since my friend and cousin, Mrs. Cheriton, came to live with me. I have been made sensible, by her sweet and gracious presence, that my life before had been very grim and solitary, and I determined that it should be so no more. I also felt that while she was spared to me it would be a happiness and a benefit to her to have some young life about the house; to have, in short, some young and sweet woman, who could be her companion in a hundred ways that would not be possible for a solitary bachelor like myself.

"With these thoughts in my mind, I naturally turned to the young women directly connected with me,—to the daughters of my brothers. I had never seen any of them; troubles into which it is not necessary for me to enter had made me withdraw until lately from all society, and I had not felt able to respond to the kind invitations sent me from time to time to visit one brother or another. I conceived the plan of sending for you three cousins to spend the summer with me, with the idea that at the end of the time I might ask one of you—the one who should seem most contented, and who should be best suited to a quiet, country life—to—a—to remain longer. This was my first plan. Perhaps it might have been better if I had adhered to it; but I subsequently modified it, not without a good deal of thought. It would be dull for you, I reflected—triste, as Rita would say,—here with me. A strange uncle, an elderly man, unused to young people, could not fail to be a constant check, a constant restraint upon gay and youthful spirits. I wanted you to be happy, so I decided to efface myself for a time, to let you have the home of your fathers for your own, unhampered by the presence of its owner."

Margaret made a motion of eager remonstrance, but her uncle checked her with raised hand.

"One moment, my dear! I now come to John Strong."

Rita raised her eyes to his, full of proud defiance.

"I deceived you!" he went on, answering her look. "I now think it was wrong, and Mrs. Cheriton, I ought to add, was opposed to the plan. But in the first place my presence here was necessary for many reasons; and in the second place I wanted to see you. I wanted to see you as you really were, not constrained or on good behaviour, or in any way changed from your own true selves. I think I succeeded."

There was a moment's silence, which none of the girls dared to break.

"My name is John Strong Montfort. I have been in the habit of spending a part of every day among my plants and flowers, for reasons of health and pleasure. It was simple enough for me to go from my private rooms to the garden, to use the private staircase which—a—with which you are familiar,"—Peggy winced and Margaret blushed, but Rita continued her direct gaze at her uncle and gave no sign,—"and to pass (by a way that has not yet been discovered) to and from the White Rooms. I intended to keep up this little farce for a few weeks only, but somehow the time has slipped by, and each day has brought you some new occupation which I was loath to interrupt. Lately, I confess, there has been a new incentive to secrecy, and perhaps—Rita—perhaps I may have been boy enough, old as I am, to enjoy my own little conspiracy. It is over; the play is played out. I have already made my peace with Margaret, and I think Peggy is prepared to accept my explanation. What do you say?"

Rita had followed every word with breathless attention, her colour coming and going, her eyes growing momently brighter. Now, at this direct appeal, she rose and flung out her arms with the dramatic gesture so familiar to two of her hearers.

"I say?" she repeated. "I say it was magnificent! It was superb! Marguerite, do I exaggerate? It was inspired! My uncle, I am prepared to adore you!"

Mr. Montfort looked alarmed, but pleased. Rita went on, glowing with enthusiasm.

"It was perfectly conceived, perfectly carried out! Ah, why were you not on my side? Together, you and I, we could have done—everything!"

"You did not ask me, my dear!" said Mr. Montfort dryly. There was that in his look that made Rita blush at last. But in her present mood she could bear anything.

"I beg again your pardon!" she cried. "Uncle, this time I beg for my own self pardon, of my own will. I was bad, wicked, abominable! Marguerite was right; she is always right! I kneel to you in penitence!"

And she would have knelt down, then and there, if her uncle had not stopped her hastily and positively.

"Give me a kiss instead, my dear!" he said. "We have had heroics enough for one day, and we must come down to plain common sense. Rita, Peggy, Margaret,—my three Margaret Montforts,—I wish and mean to love you all." He stooped and kissed each girl on the forehead; but he lingered by Margaret's side, and laid his hand on her hair with a silent gesture which held a blessing in it.

"Margaret, you must rest now!" he said with kind authority. "Rita, we have left your brother and cousin too long alone. Come with me, and let us see what we can do to make them forget their untoward introduction to Fernley House."

CHAPTER XV

FAREWELL

The days that followed were merry ones at Fernley House. Mr. Montfort insisted on treating both the young Cubans as his nephews, and found them, as he said, very pleasant lads. Carlos had something of Rita's fire, but with it a good share of common sense that kept him from folly. Fernando was a mild and gentle youth, with nothing passionate about him save his moustache, which curled with ferocity. His large, dark eyes were soft and melting, his smile pleased and apologetic; but Rita persisted in considering him a fire-eater of the most incendiary type, and enjoyed this view so much that no one had the heart to undeceive her. Altogether, the two lads made a charming addition to the party, and no one was in a hurry to break it up. Rita was to return to Cuba with her brother, but Carlos showed a most thoughtful unwillingness to hasten his sister's departure. Peggy's flaxen hair and blue eyes had been a revelation to the young man, accustomed to dark beauties all his life, and he found "Cosine Paygi" a charming companion. They were excellent friends, and when Rita and Fernando sighed and rolled their eyes (as they were very fond of doing), Peggy and Carlos laughed.

Margaret was still kept a little quiet by her hands, though the blisters were rapidly healing. The other four scampered here and there, playing hide and seek in the house, straying through the garden, dancing, singing, from morning to night. Margaret was always at hand to welcome them when they came in, to listen and laugh, or sympathise, as the case might demand. She was happy, too, in her own way, but she found herself wondering, as she had wondered before, whether she were seventeen or thirty-seven, and there was no doubt in her mind that Uncle John was nearer her in age than any of the others. Her heart was full of quiet happiness, for this dear uncle had asked her if she would stay with him, would make her home here at Fernley with him and Aunt Faith. She felt as if nothing in the world could have given her such happiness, and she shook her head, smiling, at Rita's violent protestations that she must come to Cuba, and at Peggy's equally earnest prayers that she would come out with her to the Ranch.

"Some day!" was all she could be brought to say, when her cousins hung about her with affection whose sincerity she could not doubt.

"Some day, dear girls, when Uncle John can come with me. As long as he needs me here, here I stay!"

And Peggy would pout and shake her shoulders, and Rita would fling away and call her an iceberg, a snow-queen, with marble for a heart; and two minutes after they would both be waltzing through the hall like wild creatures, calling on Margaret to observe how beautifully the boys were learning the new step.

The young men had been taken to visit Mrs. Cheriton, and came away so deeply smitten that they could talk of nothing else for some time. Rita and Peggy opened their young eyes very wide when Carlos declared she was the most beautiful person he had ever seen, and Fernando responded with fervour:

"She eess a godess! the wairld contains not of soche."

But the goddess could not dance, nor play "I spy!" and the girls soon had it their own way again.

And so the day came when the dancing and playing must stop. The day came, and the hour came; and a group, half sad, half joyful, was gathered on the stone veranda, while White Eagle stood ready at the foot of the steps, with William, waiting to drive the four travellers to the ferry. Four; for Peggy was to be met in New York by a friend and neighbour of her father's who was to take her home.

Peggy's eyes were red with weeping. Her hat was on wrong side before, and her veil was tied in a hard knot, as it had been on the night of her arrival; but Peggy did not care. She submitted while

Margaret set the hat straight; then clung round her neck, and sobbed till Carlos was quite distracted. "Margaret, I—I want to tell you!" she whispered through her tears. "I am going to be a different girl at home now. I am going to—try—to remember the way you do things, and to be a little like you. Oh, Margaret, only a little! but I want you to think that I am trying, and—and—I will remember about my buttons—and—have my boots blacked. Oh, Margaret, you have been so good to me, and I do love you so, and now I—am—going away to leave you!"

Margaret was in tears, too, by this time, seventeen having got the upper hand of thirty-seven completely.

"My dear!" she said. "My dear, darling little Peggy, I shall miss you,—oh, so much! And dear, you have taught me as much as I have taught you, and more. Think of the bog! oh, Peggy, think of the bog! and the gutter-spout! I shall never be such a coward again, and all because of you, Peggy. And we will write to each other, dear, every week, won't we? and we will always be sisters, just the same as own sisters. Good-bye, my little girl! good-bye, my dear little girl!"

The sobbing Peggy was lifted into the carriage; and now it was Rita's turn to cling about Margaret with fondest words and caresses.

"Marguerite, we part!" she said. "Très chère, how can I leave thee? I—I have learned much since I came here. We are different, yes! but I know that it is lovely to be good, though I am not good myself. You would not have me good, Marguerite? It would destroy my personnel! But I love goodness, and thee, the spirit of it. Don't shake your head, for I will not submit to it. You are good, I tell you,—good like my mother, my angel. You will think of me, chérie?—you will think of your Spanish Rita, and warm your kind, cool heart with the thought? Yes, I know you will. You will be happy here with the uncle. Yes! he's like you,—you will suit each other! For me, it would be death in two weeks; yet he is noble, he has the grand air. Très chère, I have left for you the bracelet with the rubies; it is on your toilet-table. You admired it,—it was yours from that moment, but I waited, for I knew that one day we must part. They are drops of blood, Marguerite, from my heart,—Rita's heart,—which beats ever for you. Adios, mi alma!"

All this was poured into Margaret's ear with such rapidity and fire that she could make no reply; could only embrace her cousin warmly, and promise constant thought and frequent letters.

And now Carlos was bending to kiss her hand, rather to her confusion. He regarded her with awe and veneration, and murmured that she was a lily of goodness. Fernando was saluting her with three bows, each more magnificent than the other. Mr. Montfort kissed the girls warmly, shook hands cordially with the young men.

Hands were kissed, handkerchiefs waved. Peggy, drowned in tears, looked back to utter a last farewell.

"Good-bye, Margaret! Good-bye, darling Margaret! Don't forget us!"

They were gone, and Margaret stood on the veranda and wept, her heart longing for her mates; but presently she dried her eyes, and looked up to greet her uncle with a smile.

"Dear girls!" she said; "it has been so good, so good, to have them and know them. You have given us all a great happiness, Uncle John.

And now they are going home to their own people, and that is well, too."

"And you are staying at home," said John Montfort, "with your own people. This is your home, Margaret, as long as it is mine. I cannot be your father, dear, but you must let me come as near as you can, for we have only one another,—you and Aunt Faith and I. You will stay, always, will you not, to be our light and comfort? I don't feel as if I could ever let you go again."

"Oh," said Margaret, and her eyes ran over again with happy tears, "Oh, if I can really be a comfort, Uncle, I shall be so glad—so glad! but I know so little! I am—"

But Uncle John had only one word to say, and that was the one word of an old song that he loved, and that his mother had sung to him when he was a little lad in the nursery:

> "Weel I ken my ain lassie;
> Kind love is in her e'e!"

THE END